Dating Game

By Erik Schubach

Chapter 1 – The Breakup

I was desperate to cheer Beverly up after that bitch Lori had unceremoniously dumped her for some vapid pillow princess, Bev and Lori had been together for over six months, a record relationship when it came to Beverly. The girl had the propensity for the "Love 'em and leave 'em." lifestyle, but I seriously thought things with Lori were going to work out for her. She had finally got serious about someone, though Lori was extremely pushy, controlling and demanding. I never thought I'd see the day when a girl tamed my best friend.

But now, here I am, left picking up the pieces of her first heartbreak. Bevi and I had been best friends since before I can actually remember. With us living next door to each other since we were toddlers, it was only obvious that we'd gravitate to each other.

As we grew up, the entire neighborhood knew us as Beverly and Crystal, double trouble. Wherever one was, the other was sure to follow.

Early on, she had bestowed me with the nickname Krustallos, or Kru for short. I, of course, had no clue at the time what it meant, so I retaliated by christening her with the nickname she still shudders at today, Bevi. Of course, now I know that krustallos is Greek for crystal, but didn't know it back then.

I was always the shorter, shy and more reserved one, with my signature chestnut tresses and my single blue eye that sparkled like my namesake, my other eye, green as a result of my heterochromia iridium. My unusual eyes polarized people, either they loved them or they thought they were freaky.

Now Bev... she was the yang to my yin. A tall and lanky, fiery freckled redhead with emerald green eyes, who was outgoing, boisterous and fearless. Ready to take on the world and make it hers.

She was a fierce friend who wouldn't back down from anything to protect me. We were inseparable in school. I was a late bloomer but nobody teased me because of that or my strange eyes, they knew they'd suffer Beverly's wrath if they dared. Just ask Kenny Watkins. *Shudder.*

It was near the end of our freshman year of high school after Scott Taylor had asked me to the Spring Fling school dance that Bev had pulled me to the side with the most serious look I had ever seen on her face.

Her eyes pleaded with mine to hear her out, in one of our silent conversations complete with point and counter point that we'd had this innate ability to read in each other for as long as I could remember. It ended in me silently bidding her to continue and not to worry so much.

That's when she came out to me, she was terrified as she spoke, "Krustallos... Kru... I need to tell you something. I don't want you to find out from somebody else, or when we go to the dance... but I'm scared you are going to hate me." She was shifting her weight from side to side nervously which of course caused me to subconsciously reach up to fidget with the end of my trademark, high, sloppy ponytail.

She was scaring me as I spoke, "Bevi, you're kind of freaking me out. Find out what?" I searched her shocking green eyes with my blue and green, trying to conjure the answer from their depths. She took a deep breath and opened her mouth to start, but shut it and paused, looking at me. I gave her a reassuring but nervous smile.

She straightened and smiled her patented lopsided smile and started, "I'm thinking on asking Wendy Timms to the dance." She found her shoes extremely fascinating suddenly as she continued, "Kru... Crystal... I... I like girls. I'm gay," finally rushed out of her mouth. She looked back up at me and shied away in a motion like she was expecting someone to strike her.

I blinked at her and exhaled the breath I didn't know I was holding as I dropped my hand from my hair in relief. Then I laughed. "Oh, that? God Bev, I thought you were going to tell me you were dying or something. Don't ever scare me like that again!"

It wasn't often that I could shock Beverly, but there she was just standing in front of me with her mouth hanging open, stunned. I almost laughed again at the sight.

She shook her head once and looked at me in confusion, "You... you knew?"

I rolled my eyes at her and smiled, "Duh. Like you could hide something like that from me. I've seen the signs and the clues over the past couple years."

She blinked rapidly at me again putting all the pieces together, "You knew? You didn't say anything? And you're not mad? You don't hate me?"

I laughed at her, putting my hand on her shoulder like I always did and gave it a little squeeze and said, "Of course I don't hate you, your my fracking best friend, I love your sorry ass. Why would I be mad? Who the hell cares which two people like each other? Aaaaaaand... with your hot self off the market, it just leaves more boys for me." I waggled my eyebrows at her.

Instantly I was in a bone crushing hug with her speaking over my shoulder, "One, don't ever use those lame SciFi cuss words again. And two, why the hell didn't you say anything, brat? I've been stressing about this moment for months!"

I shrugged and spoke matter of factly, "I just assumed you knew that I knew."

She broke the hug, shaking her head in amusement and looking at me like I was crazy. "You're damn lucky I love you too or I'd kick your ass for making me do this."

After that, our roles in the school kind of reversed, I was the one defending her once the school found out about her liking girls. I mean, how immature can high school kids be? Donna Barnes found out the hard way never to call Bev a dyke when I was within earshot. It was worth my two day suspension to feed her own teeth to her.

Of course, the inevitable rumors circulated that Bev and I were lesbian lovers. I didn't pay much attention since it didn't matter. Even if it were true, then hey, I'd have a smokin' hot girlfriend and how could that possibly be a bad thing? Bevi brought up on more than one occasion that she loved that I couldn't care less about anyone's sexual orientation, that more people should have my attitude.

The rumors faded over the years as Bev started dating as many gay girls as she could find in the school, she had even stole a couple straight girls away from some of the jocks.

With my new confidence, being Bev's protector, I was on quite the dating spree myself. It seemed like the boys lined up to date me, in no small part to get close to my hot lesbian best friend. *What tools!*

It was in our senior year, on one of our weekly sleepovers, we were both between relationships. We were reminiscing about our friendship and everything we had been through together. Sexuality came up and heavy questions about how one knows if they are gay or straight or none or all of the above were discussed. My openness to the idea that most of it was more of a fluid, gray and fuzzy line, even though most people fooled themselves into believing it was black and white, piqued her interest.

That's when she asked me, "Kru, you ever fancy a girl? Or even been curious?"

I thought for a second and shrugged. "Yeah, sometimes I have like, girl crushes, but I'm sure that's normal. But I do really crush on guys more. Ever since I realized you were gay, I've always been curious, but never curious enough to test the waters. I find women and men sexy, but just never leaned far enough over the 'fuzzy gray' since I haven't been disappointed with dating guys yet."

She got suddenly shy and looked at me innocently. "You... you want to try? Like, with me? Just experiment, I mean?"

This piqued my own curiosity, but I hid it for a chance to tease her, "What? Bev? Do you like me?"

She held her hands up in defense. "No, I don't mean like that, well maybe, well I don't know. But I mean, like, you can just test the waters with me to see if you like it. With someone you can trust. It's only an experiment after all."

I grinned at my success in flustering her, then I shrugged again and locked eyes with her and leaned half way into her. She hesitantly closed the gap. Our lips were an inch apart and she shot me a questioning look with her eyes. *Indecisive much, Bevi?* I rolled my eyes at her sudden timidness and closed the gap and kissed her desperately, trying to feel passion.

I had seriously been curious if I could possibly be gay or bi for the past year or two. Any type of sexuality really doesn't bug me. But this was not the sexy, sensual, passionate experience I had envisioned in kissing a girl. We both pulled back smacking our own lips like we had just eaten something distasteful.

"Ewww." Bev said.

I scrunched up my face and agreed, "Yeah, eww. That was seriously like kissing my own sister. Now I feel like I had just attempted incest." I shuddered. She nodded in agreement, wiping her lips multiple times. Our eyes making a non-verbal pact *NEVER* to try that again.

"So, I take it you're not going to be riding the rainbow?" She laughed out.

I nodded, trying to suppress my own laughter. "Yeah, guess that certifies me as straight. For some reason I'm a little disappointed about that. I would make a hot lez." It was her turn to shrug with a smirk as she recalled our conversation from years back. "Yeah, but with your hot self off the market, it just leaves more girls for me." We shared a giggle.

Fast forward six years to today and we are still the best of friends. After college I started my own business as an upscale party planner here in Redmond, Washington, and am making a very comfortable living. Since my hours are so lax with a huge monetary return, I get plenty of time to party with Bev, who is now the premiere convention planner here in the Seattle area.

Last night I woke up to the sound of a key in the lock of my condominium, I wasn't alarmed as there is only one other person with a key. A moment later a disheveled Bevi came walking into my bedroom. I could see her mascara running down her cheeks and her eyes puffy and red from crying, even in the dim illumination from the nightlight by the bedroom door.

She looked at me like a beat puppy. It wasn't hard for me to fathom what had happened. I wordlessly raised my covers invitingly and she slid into the queen sized bed with her back to me.

I pulled her into me and just stroked her hair and held her as she cried herself to sleep on my pillow. I knew there would be time enough to talk in the morning. Right now my best friend just needed comfort. I was already cursing Lori's name in my head, I never liked that controlling bitch.

Early the next morning I quietly started to get up, but as I untangled myself from Bev, she grabbed my arm and pulled me back into the big spoon position, my arm protectively wrapped around her waist.

"Not yet, sis." she said sleepily.

I kissed the top of her head, smiling. "Just let me know when you are ready."

A few minutes later, the sun was sneaking through the window and warming us. Bevi stretched like a jungle cat, making a satisfied sound.

"Ahhhh... thanks Kru, I needed a Crystal recharge." She spun around on the bed to face me with a silly grin, "Me hungry." She pouted like a little kid as I laughed and slid out of the bed and wandered out the door.

I returned a few seconds later, she had wiped much of the makeup damage off with some tissue. I tossed one of the two chocolate pudding cups I was holding to her. She deftly caught it with one hand.

"Mmmm... my favorite!" she said.

We pulled the foil tops off and just started licking the contents out of the cups without spoons. Nothing was said until we had licked the cups dry, completing our breakup ritual.

She tossed me the empty and I round filed them beside my

computer desk as she stood and wandered toward the bathroom, not shutting the door. I followed and sat on the toilet seat as she started up the shower and began stripping. I prompted her, "So spill girl, do I need to go over and mess Lori up?"

She looked at me through the mirror as she examined her own naked form in it. She, like me, had a slight figure and smallish breasts, but like all things, it isn't quantity, it's quality. I've always thought she looked statuesque with her cute girl next door (literally) face, and that wild mane of red hair coupled with her veil of freckles that drove many a woman crazy with lust.

She finally spoke, her voice husky, on the verge of crying, "She kicked me out last night when I caught her with that Candice ditz, you know 'Candy' the barista from the coffee shop? I walk in, and there's Lori munching away at that pillow princess, then she has the nerve to scream at *ME* for walking in on them. I mean, what the hell?"

I was clenching my fists and I saw her eyes drop to them in the mirror.

"Don't do anything Kru. I still love her, even tho she made it quite clear we are over. This is so messed up. This is why I vowed to never fall in love. I mean, the one time I do, look at what happens. Only one night stands for me from now on." She wandered into the shower as we spoke and pulled the curtain shut.

"At least let me take Candy down a few pegs." I called out to her, and I heard her giggle.

She replied, "No, it isn't her fault. She's got the IQ of a thumbtack and will spread her legs for anyone. I swear she wouldn't get any if she wasn't a stone cold fifteen out of ten. I mean seriously, even you almost orgasm when she smiles at you. I'm sure she didn't even realize Lori was supposedly in a committed relationship."

I heard the soft crying over her false bravado. I waited, letting her get it all out again. I hated this, I hated Lori, I hated the fact that Bev was right about Candy. But nobody should be able to make my best friend cry.

I heard her sniff and knew she was gathering her wits. "You didn't turn my room into like a sex dungeon or a mini golf course yet did you? She kinda gave me till the weekend to get my stuff out."

I laughed out loud, "Well your room kind of *IS* a sex dungeon hon, it's exactly how you left it five months ago when you moved in with Lori."

She popped her wet head out from behind the shower curtain with a grin, though I knew she was just pretending to be brave, and she said, "Awwww... you missed me!"

I laughed. "No, I'm just too lazy to throw your crap out." I winked at her. "Really though Bevi, you know that you *ALWAYS* have a room with me."

Her brave facade cracked a little, she sniffed then she walked out of the shower leaving it running, and leaned down to hug me, getting my bed clothes all wet. Then she grabbed a towel off the rack and started drying herself. I couldn't stop myself from smiling. "You really gotta do something about your overwhelming shyness and modesty, Bev."

This got the desired laugh from her as she wandered out to get some clothes from her room as I started stripping and stepped into the still running shower to prep for the day. Coming up with a plan to cheer her up and get her over Lori.

- - -

That afternoon I went to get little miss mopey butt out of her room, she had been barricaded in there most of the day. "Ok, get yer sorry ass gussied up. We're hitting Ballyhoo tonight!" This brought a flicker of excitement to her face, but I could also see the shadow of sadness over Lori in her eyes.

The Ballyhoo Club was an elite lesbian bar in downtown Seattle, with live music and a large dance floor. It leaned heavily toward the lipstick side of the lesbian spectrum. It was one of our stomping grounds before Lori tamed my Bev. We would alternate between Ballyhoo and straight clubs like the Steam Plant Club to make hookups. Taking turns on being the others wingman.

One of our favorite rundowns at the Ballyhoo was what we had deemed 'The Bruiser'. We'd sit on opposite sides of the bar and I would complain to the hottest girl around me, pointing out Bev and warning the girl to stay away from her. That we had hooked up one night last week and she wouldn't stop after I lost count of the orgasms and passed out, and that I'd been bruised down below all week because of that night. All that pleasure just wasn't worth it. We'd time it to see just how quickly the girl would wind up by her side, buying her a drink.

The straight bars were even easier since guys are such horn dogs. She'd just sit suggestively close to me giving me adoring looks, usually with her hand resting on my arm, stroking it, cooing in my ear. We'd be swarmed with men almost instantly and I could basically have my pick of the litter. God, we were bad girls.

Though the past year it had been almost pure Ballyhoo until Bev found Lori; I've just gotten tired of the whole hookup scene. Maybe I'm maturing, but I've sort of been wanting a real relationship lately, and the clubs are not a place to find something other than a one night stand. I've *NEVER* made it past a second date before. But on the same token, I'm also in no real hurry to find someone. I'm pretty satisfied with the way my life is going right now.

An hour later we both strutted out of our rooms and appraised each other. She was decked out to the nines, in a sassy short red dress that made for easy access. I didn't see any panty line. *That's it, my best friend is a certified slut.* Her four inch red stilettos and thigh high black lace, nylon stockings were a perfect compliment to the 'please do me' dress.

Her delicate dangling earring and necklace brought your attention to her face. As usual her eyes were made up all smoky and seductive and she had clear lip gloss adoring her lips in case a kissing emergency came up. Better to not leave a mark if kissing a girl who doesn't wear your shade. About thirty two trillion bangle bracelets adorned each wrist to complete the look.

I was in pretty much my everyday clothes, a tight pair of low cut capri jeans that ended half way down my calf. Simple black socks with my black and white converse on my feet. My white midriff tank tee showed off a teasing amount of my flat stomach. Just a hint of eye and lip makeup and my hair up in my ever present, sloppy high ponytail with locks of escaped hair drifting across my dual color eyes to finish my look.

This was our practiced Ballyhoo look, always making sure we both looked nice, but with my tall (even taller in her heels) best friend looking more stunning and refined. Ensuring that all the action would go her way. This both freed me from the endless turndowns with the explanation I was straight (unless we were doing a rundown), and assured her a hookup.

"Ten." I said in smiling appraisal and nodding up at her.

"Nine." she responded with a smile of her own down to me.

With that ritual completed, we shared a chuckle and locked arms then marched out the door to the car for the short ride across Lake Washington into Seattle.

Chapter 2 – The Ballyhoo

After parking a block away, we marched up to the Ballyhoo. The line stretched half way down the block and we went straight past it right up to the heavyset woman sitting on a stool manning the door, Minnie. She was tough looking; but still managed to ooze more femininity than someone of her stature should. Bev and I have always liked her. She was a genuine nice lady.

I placed my hand gently on her arm and she turned to me with a huge smile.

"Crystal! Beverly! Oh my God, I haven't seen you two since forever!" she said in a gravelly smoker's voice.

I smiled and idly rubbed my thumb on her surprisingly muscular arm as I responded, "Yeah Bevi here got herself in a real relationship so we've been a little scarce. But now, we're here to mend her broken heart, or at least give it a cardio workout." She chuckled at that.

Minnie reached over and gave Bev a quick reassuring squeeze on her arm. "Don't worry hon, you'll find someone." Then she turned to me, "Speaking of. Still straight?"

I laughed. "Far as I can tell, sorry, Minnie."

She grinned back at me with eyes twinkling in humor. "Such a waste. Well you girls go in and have a fun time."

I bent down and kissed her on the cheek. "Thanks, Min. Talk to you later."

We heard girls in the line grumbling about us getting in before them and I caught Minnie's smile turn to a frown as she admonished the people in line. Bev laughed when she heard the commotion and said, "I have no clue how you get away with all that teasing with her, sis. But not complaining, I hate waiting in line."

I rolled my eyes. "It's all in the delivery. And hey, you know just as well as I do that she's a nice lady!" Bev just smiled and said, "True dat." I winced, "Never say that again."

We quickly made our way through the sea of women, and the occasional man, toward the bar as was our custom. Drinks first, poach a table second. With those two prerequisites procured then it is dancing, having a good time, and getting Bev a hookup. I was happy to see all eyes were on her as we passed, letting us know my dress-down was working, as always.

Just as we were reaching the bar, Bev shot me a look in our

silent communication, flickering her eyes toward a couple girls at a table gathering their purses. Like a well oiled machine we peeled off in two directions. She stood at the table as they left and slid into a seat just as I arrived at the bar. *Bam! That's how it's done folks!*

I raised a hand and got the attention of Maggie, the bartender. She smiled and rushed over to the complaint of some of the girls that were there before me and said, "Hey Crystal! Long time no see! The usual?" I nodded with a smile.

Maggie was great, she was a wizard behind the bar and as straight as they came. But the clientele didn't mind because she was just a naturally flirtatious girl who made sure to never lead anyone on. She was just a very likeable person, period.

I glanced around for possible targets for Bev. I got a couple appraising looks and one shy smile from some of the girls at the bar myself as I waited.

Maggie slid a couple vodka shots and beer chasers over to me, and entered it on her tablet computer under my account.

She smiled as she said, "Have a great time! Have Bev come say hi when she's not too busy making girls walk funny, OK?" I nodded with a laugh as I could actually visualize what she had just described.

"Will do Mags!" I said cheerfully as I skillfully balanced the glasses as I wandered over to Bev, who had already turned away a couple girls who had tried to sit with her.

"I forgot how much of a meat market this place is!" She shouted over the music with her lopsided smile.

We both knocked back our shots and chugged half our beer and smacked them on the table with a satisfying clunk, causing the golden liquid in them to slosh around. I smirked at her comment and leaned in. "Well they're not here to talk! Oh, and don't forget to say hi to Maggie tonight sometime!" I yelled. She smiled and nodded in understanding.

We both looked around as we laid our light jackets and hung our purses on the backs of our chairs, claiming the table. Then we relaxed away from each other and limited eye contact so the ladies would know that we were not together. As was our custom, we did a cursory scan of the club looking for any obvious targets for Bev.

On the other side of the dance floor, I caught a striking brunette looking our way. Even from this distance I could tell that her eyes were dark pools of chocolate brown. She had a look of laid back confident interest. *The girl has charisma, that's for sure!* She was dressed much the same as I was but she definitely made the look work better than me. I tilted my head and toyed with the end of my ponytail as I saw her gracefully turn down a girl who had approached her table. I mentally tagged her to point out to Bev, since the brunette was showing obvious interest in her.

There was the usual mix in attendance tonight. Some girls were there simply for dancing and a good time, some looking for a hookup, straight girls who are in the curious and experimental stage, and the occasional guy. Most of the ladies tolerated the guys in here so long as they didn't try hitting on anyone. They had to be accompanied by a girl when they came in or they would be turned away at the door.

Most guys usually came with a lesbian friend just for moral support and sometimes for the dancing. If they were just looking to 'score', thinking they could 'turn' a lesbian because they had just 'never been with a real man', they'd find themselves thrown out on their butt by Minnie or one of the two male bouncers (the only men that worked here). The girl that brought the guy would be banned from the club. I had never personally seen this happen but from what I hear, it is a pretty funny sight.

I saw a couple more potential girls to point out to Bev as the band started into a kick ass hip hop cover. Bevi and I smiled at each other and headed for the dance floor. *God I love dancing!* I just bopped my head to the beat and swayed my arms over my head, swiveling my hips and singing at the top of my lungs. Bev followed suit, but she would occasionally turn and grind suggestively with random girls around her without breaking eye contact with me.

She could work the crowd like nobody's business, and look damn good doing it. I was happy to see that her smile was finally reaching her eyes again. I know it will take some time for her to really get over Lori, but at least we were getting her to forget about it for the night.

I glanced over at the far table and that cute brunette was eyeballing Bev again with a hungry smile. Wow, the girl was even more striking with that smile on her face. *I'll have to move her up on Bevi's priority list.*

We returned to the table when the song ended, laughing and feeling energized. I winked in conspiracy at Bev. "Ok, I'll mosey off for a bit to set the 'empty chair' bait for you at the table here and see if I can't go generate more interest for ya!" I yelled over the music. She offered her lopsided grin in understanding as I wandered off toward the bar.

Remembering the brunette at the last second, I veered off and made my way around the dance floor toward her table. Maybe I could help speed things along for Bev. I caught Maggie's attention with a smile as I walked past and held up two fingers and pointed toward Bev. She nodded with a grin and started prepping more drinks to have delivered to our table. I was liking my gentle buzz and wasn't ready to loose it just yet.

I approached the brunette who seemed to be watching me approach and I smiled big at her cute as hell grin. I got close and leaned in to yell above the music. "Hi! Mind if I sit?"

She yelled, "Hi! I fucking love your eyes!" with a stunning smile as she motioned to the empty chair beside her.

Smiling back, I took a seat and leaned in close to be heard over the music. "So I noticed you've been checking out my friend, Bev, over there! I just thought I'd let you know that we're not together, so you might wanna ask her to dance!"

She looked at me with a 'that's just silly' kind of crooked smile, it was almost cartoon like, then she pursed her lips and yelled back. "I wasn't checking *HER* out." Then she smiled a butterfly in the belly materializing smile at me.

I blushed a little and dropped my eyes slightly. "Oh. I'm sorry. I'm straight. I just came to lend moral support for my best friend there. You know, do a little wingman thing? I didn't mean to lead you on or anyth..." I was cut off by her lips on mine. To my surprise I found myself returning the kiss. *This is nice!* It was absolutely nothing like kissing Bev and not at all like kissing a sister.

My butterflies doubled as she broke the kiss, leaving me with my eyes closed. *I don't even remember closing them.*

She shouted. "Sorry, it was the only thing I could think of to shut you up. You were babbling and not letting me cut in."

I opened my eyes and smiled warmly at her. "No worries, it was nice."

She raised a perfectly sculpted eyebrow as she replied, obviously a little surprised that I didn't freak out. "Are you *SURE* you're straight?"

I glanced at the dance floor and saw Bev out there almost having sex with a hot 'Barbie' blonde in the middle of it. This made me smile for her. I turned back to the girl still smiling and shouted, "Pretty sure, my best friend there and I tested the theory before, but it was like kissing my sister." Then I extended my hand to her with a genuine smile. "Crystal, by the way!"

She shook my hand and I swear an electric current passed between us. "Riley! Ahhh... forget I said that... everyone calls me Jane!" she shouted. Then she tilted her head a bit and got a curious look on her face. "So was kissing me like kissing your sister?"

I had to seriously think on that as I shook my head slowly. "No. It was actually quite enjoyable." She still seemed shocked that I seemed comfortable with my sexuality, no matter how ambiguous it was looking at that particular moment in time.

"Crystal, you ever think that you felt like you were kissing your sister because you see your friend *AS* your sister?" She inquired.

Hmm... Riley is full of good questions.

I looked at her thoughtfully, really contemplating it. "You know, I never thought about that before. Huh. Who knows, I could be gay and just never knew because of that one experience." I shrugged. "But I do think that I enjoy the company of men more."

She looked shocked at my truthfulness and I'm sure also about the fact that it didn't really seem to matter one way or the other to me. *It doesn't.* She smiled and asked, "Even after this epiphany?"

I grinned at her and shrugged, seriously considering the question.

I noticed a guy walking past the table with some drinks I grabbed his shirt as he passed and pulled him down to my lips and kissed him similar to the way Riley had just kissed me. He almost dropped the drinks, his eyes wide.

I let go of his shirt then yelled, "Shoo!" to him, making a dismissive motion with my hand and he wandered off to his original destination in smiling confusion. Riley looked half shocked and half amused.

She was about to say something when I surprised her by grabbing her tank top and pulling her into another comparison kiss. She seemed to melt in this time, she tasted good. I melted a bit too if I'm to be completely honest with myself.

I released her and licked my lips, leaving her gasping with wide eyes on mine. I thought hard for a second while she tried to form words, then I yelled, "I don't know. You are definitely a *MUCH* better kisser, and your lips are so soft, but I think I still like strength of a male against my lips. So I'd say it is a tossup, but men barely win. Unless of course all women kiss like you."

Her eyes were darting all over me I could see the wheels turning in her head. I broke eye contact for a second and caught a glimpse of Bevi dragging the blonde away toward the restroom. *Score!* I turned my attention back to Riley and for some reason, she seemed a *LOT* more interesting to me than she was before. She was definitely hot, any other straight girl would agree.

She finally spoke with a mischievous grin, "Just as well, I'm sure you'd be a terrible date. All that straight confusion bouncing around in your head."

I took mock offense and defended myself, "Hey! Watch it! I give good date! A lot better than you could manage!" I winked playfully at her.

She arched that perfectly sculpted eyebrow again. *God her eyes were entrancing.* "One of my dates and you'd be my bitch!" she challenged with a cute smirk.

This girl intrigued me, and she was fun and confident. *Let's knock her off her game.*

I smiled seductively. "Ok! Let's test your theory! I suggest a wager! We each get a chance to take the other on a date. Then whoever's date was the better date wins the bet and the loser has to stand on that bar and announce to the club that the other made her their bitch!" I finished by pointing at the bar, my eyebrow cocked in challenge, a slight smirk at the corner of my lip.

She looked both surprised and excited about this prospect and prompted, "But you're straight! That would mean going on two dates with a girl!"

I rolled my eyes with a playful grin. "I'm not that insecure about my sexuality. Are you? It's not like we're having sex or anything!"

She just shot a stunning smile that made me start fussing with the end of my ponytail and biting my lower lip as she yelled, "It's a bet!"

I took her hand and shook it, holding on just a little too long, I really enjoyed the warmth of our contact.

It was her turn to bite her lower lip, and I'd have to say it was one of the most adorable things I had ever seen. The band started a slow cover of 'We Shall' by Mandy Fay Harris. *I love this song!* Riley leaned in to my ear. "Seal it with a dance?"

I nodded enthusiastically and allowed her to drag me to the dance floor. I had this sudden desire to be close to her.

She was taller than me so she rested her arms on my shoulder as I rested mine on her hips. We didn't speak we just swayed and turned with the music. I wanted contact so I laid my head in the crook of her neck, our chests coming in contact. I heard her inhale sharply. I was all abuzz but relaxed at the same time. I felt her head rest gently on top of mine. I smiled. *I like being short at times like this.*

As the song was winding down I noticed Bev dancing with her very content and satisfied looking blonde nearby. She was looking between Riley and I and mouthing, "Oh my God!" to me. I just smiled at her as Riley led me around in a final lazy circle.

We stayed out on the floor for the next couple cover songs; one pop, the other hip hop, this band was kickin'. We laughed, smiled, and sang throughout it, just generally having a good time. I was pleasantly surprised that she could keep up with my moves. Her own moves were mesmerizing in their own right... I caught myself licking my lips on more than one occasion. *Hmmm.*

When the next song started I grabbed her hand and dragged her to Bev at our table to catch our breath. I was having more fun than I have had in a long time. We sat with Bev and the blonde, then I caught the attention of a passing server, Amy, and just held up four fingers. She winked at me and ran off to the bar. *It's good to know everyone here.*

The music volume was dropping as the night had been rolling along, the subtle way that clubs slowly wind down the night over the hours. So we could talk at slightly elevated levels instead of yelling at this point. I made an introduction, "Beverly, I'd like you to meet Jane. Riley I'd like you to meet Bev, my bestest and most dear friend." They exchanged smiles and shook hands.

Bev was still looking between us in shock as she spoke, "Jane and Crystal, I'd like you to meet Tara." The blonde offered quickly, "Trish." with an evil glare at Bev.

"I mean Trish." Bev corrected herself.

It was soooo hard for me not to laugh and I saw Riley having the same problem, squishing her head to her shoulders.

Shots and chasers arrived and we all downed them with ease. "So Bevi, Riley here thinks she can arrange a better date than I can."

Bev laughed, knowing my connections because of my job. I saw her eyebrow quirk when I called her Riley.

The brunette caught this and said to me, "I told you everyone calls me Jane."

I played with my ponytail as I bit my lower lip and said as innocently and cutely as I could, "I'm not everybody, Riley." I squinted my eyes with a smile when I said her name again.

"Jesus! You gotta stop doing stuff like that." Riley exclaimed, licking her lips, breathing raggedly.

I perked up a little at a thought. "So, why do they call you Jane? Middle name?"

She shrugged. "I really have no clue, someone called me that in the first grade. Maybe they thought I was someone else, but other people overheard and it just sorta stuck. Never liked my first name and my middle name is Winfred so I never complained."

I smiled at this revelation. "Well, I happen to think Riley suits you." I dismissed it before she could argue and turned to Bev and said, "Anyway, we made ourselves a wager. We each take the other out on our best date, and whoever set up the best date wins. Loser announces, standing on the bar, that the other girl made them their bitch."

Bev shot a look of concern to Riley and said, "Ooooo... sorry

Jane, but hey, at least you'll have fun."

Riley smirked, then laughed before she responded confidently, "Don't be so sure about the outcome."

God she oozed charisma.

Bevi turned to me screwing up her face in comical confusion, "But wait. How's this supposed to work when you're straight as an arrow, Kru?"

I shrugged, not taking my eyes off of Riley's as I spoke to my friend, "Well you know me. It won't bother me if it doesn't bother her. And I'm thinking I may be a little bendy now anyway after the knee buckler she laid on me earlier."

Bev's eyes shot wide at this admission. "No way!" she mouthed.

We exchanged information and solidified the terms of our gentlewoman's agreement. I'd be up first tomorrow night, a Friday, and she got the following Saturday. I asked for her dress and shoe size cryptically. She endlessly tried finding out why, but I reminded her of the rule that we had, to go along with whatever the person setting up the date said.

Then the three of us spent the rest of the night chatting and joking and laughing. Tina... I mean Tara... no, ummm... Trish! Had left early on with some friends, realizing she had almost nothing to add to our conversations. I kind of felt bad about it; but she did come for a hookup just like Bev and from what Bevi says, they did... twice.

It was fun finding out a few things about Riley. She was a small plane pilot, who flew a Cessna 205, and ran a one person air tour company with some high class clients that ran in the same circles as my clientele. This could be useful in the future for my party planning and vice versa. Maybe we could send referrals to each other. *Nice! An excuse to hang around with this fascinating girl sometime!*

On the drive home, Bev accused me of having eye sex with Riley the whole night. I shrugged. Maybe I was. Bevi seemed extremely excited about it. I just rolled my eyes and smiled.

Chapter 4 – First Date

When the next morning rolled around, I contacted a few places to set up the date. I had a great plan. I was excited to hang out with Riley again, and I of course wanted to win. Truth be told, if we based it off of the fun from last night alone, I had already lost. I simply loved dancing and speaking with her! So I'll have to step up my game a bit here.

I didn't have any parties to start planning until Tuesday so I buckled down and dedicated my entire focus on tonight. I know it was supremely short notice but I pulled in a few markers; networking is great, it's what I do, it's what I love. The dress and shoes should be expressed to her at 5:00pm and I'd be picking her up at 6:30 for our dinner.

Around lunch my phone buzzed, I checked the text message, it was from Riley. *[bored]* I laughed and replied, *[call me]*.

Moments later the phone was ringing with her caller ID, I answered, "Hey girl! Why you so bored?"

She laughed. "Hey! Don't have a flight until 2:30. I really don't think I can read the same four, ten year old car magazines here at the hangar again."

I smiled at this as I pictured it in my head before I responded, "Well, just chat with me while I make a snack for lunch then. I can try to be more interesting than reading about which cars have a more efficient turbo." This got me the desired laugh from her, tinkling like wind chimes.

I multi-tasked, making two hot ham and cheese sandwiches, sending emails and instant messages from my iPad to prep for tonight, and just chatting, joking and laughing with Riley. *She's so easy to talk to.* Bev materialized from her moping dungeon and wandered over to take the second sandwich I had sitting on a little plate for her at the edge of the counter, and wandered back into her cave.

"What you scarfing down? Sounds good by the satisfied grunts you are making," Riley said in a tone tinged with mirth.

"Just a sandwich," I said.

She lowered her voice to a conspiratorial tone, "Describe it for me, I had a stupid granola bar and a water. Let me live my lunch vicariously through you."

I snickered at that and replied with a smile. "Well I grilled... on marbled rye of course, some thick slices of honey ham, with a generous slice of pepper jack cheese. Slathered it with a homemade creamy au-jus sauce. Oh, and one sweet pickle on the side. Has to be sweet, I hate dill pickles!"

She gasped dramatically, "Damn. I think I just had a food-gasm. Not only are you a box tease, but now you're a food tease too!"

I couldn't stop the snort that this evoked from me as I defended myself. "Hey! You told me to describe it. And for full disclosure, you think just hearing about it can give you a food-gasm, you should taste it! Mmmmm." This elicited a, "Tease, tease, tease..." causing us both to laugh.

We went on talking until 2:00 when regrettably she said, "Hey Cryster, gotta go prep and preflight the Cessna. Clients will be here in a bit."

Reluctantly I agreed. "Ok, fine. I gotta finish prepping the winning date anyway." This got me an, "In your dreams girl. Bye."

I smiled huge. "Bye!" I ended the call. I tingled a bit at the new nickname she had just bestowed upon me, haven't heard that one yet.

Crap! I had to make a couple last minute calls to complete the planning, that call ate up a lot of time. *But it was so much fun! I'd rather be talking to her.*

Around 3:00 I Google Mapped her address so I could enter it into the GPS in my phone for when I went to pick her up. When I saw she was in a loft by Pioneer Square, a smile crept up on my lips. *Oooo... I got another idea.* I dialed up another contact.

"Hi, Fredrick? Yeah it's me Crystal. What? Oh you flatterer. I need a huge favor tonight. No *YOU* still owe *ME* one. Remember the Flannery bash I secured for you in April? Yeah, thought so. Think I could borrow you and Flower tonight for a date? Yeah I know it's short notice. What? Oh no, it's a really nice girl. How would you know which way I swing? So can I? Ok thanks. This just about makes us even. I'll text you the address, 6:30 pm sharp. Yes thanks, bye!"

I did a geeky victory dance and called around to shuffle things so they still worked for the 9:00 pm surprise before I started getting ready for the date. Bevi wandered into my room as I started sliding into my dark green evening gown with matching four inch suede heels, she didn't look as depressed as she was earlier today.

"So, you seem to be putting a lot of effort into this date. You sure there isn't something you want to tell me?" She asked with a mischievous lopsided grin.

I slapped her arm and just turned around and grabbed my hair in my hands exposing my neck. People seem to think it is scary just how in synch Bev and I are, we just see it as how it has always been. She reached absently for the pearl necklace on my dressing table and draped it around me as she worked the clasp.

I shrugged as she started brushing out my hair and pulled it into a high ponytail, being sure to leave a lock out to fall over my face as I spoke, "It's just a bet. She insulted my dating ability."

I saw Bev cock an eyebrow in the mirror, saying, "Ok. Whatever you say. I just don't want to see you hurt, sis. We'd have to start stocking up on pudding cups."

We shared a laugh at that as I put in some matching pearl earrings. Bev looked at me and the dress and raised a finger then ran out of the room. That was her "Ah-ha!" face, wonder what she's up to. I started putting on my makeup when she returned and started fussing with my ponytail. She's always said it was my best asset.

We finished and I turned my head to see the ponytail in the mirror. She had taken some dark green felted Christmas ribbon that matched the dress and fashioned a bow at the knot of the ponytail and then put several thin curled strips of silver ribbon draping down from it to my shoulders. "Perfect Bevi!" I exclaimed.

She replied with a cocky grin. "Yes, I know I am," getting another arm slap and a chuckle from me.

I stood and twirled for inspection. "Ten." she said with a grin.

I took in her flannel pajamas, messy hair and looked slightly up into her red, cried out eyes. *Woohoo I'm almost as tall as her when I'm in heels!*

"Six." I responded in our ritual, offering sympathy for my truthful appraisal of her in this state.

She dumped my purse and put my wallet, keys and phone into a silver clutch then shooed me out the door.

I hopped on the 520 for the twenty minute drive into Seattle. I caught myself fidgeting with the end of my ponytail and instead punched up Riley on speakerphone.

She answered, "What the hell is this dress?"

I giggled and replied, "And hello to you too. I'm 'bout a half hour out, I'll be there 6:30 on the dot. You almost ready, lady?"

She sheepishly replied, "Well if I'm going to be completely honest, then I've been ready for like a half hour. Not that I'd actually admit that to you or anything. So really, what gives with the dress and heels?"

I smiled, she was like a dog with a bone and wouldn't let go. So I sighed in defeat.

"Well, most people only see the relaxed party girl side of me, but half my life is spent in a different world. The fantasies I create for people with my party planning. I just thought I'd give you a glimpse into that other side of me," I said more truthfully than I was willing to admit to myself.

She sounded odd, "So, like how many guys have you done this with? Is it your typical first date?" I took a deep breath ready to just dodge the question, but my traitorous mouth told the truth again. "Actually, this is the first time I've ever let anyone see this part of me outside of Bev." I got a quiet, "Oh." from her.

There was an awkward silence that followed that, unlike our smooth conversations from earlier so I just started talking. "Truth be told, I've never made it past a second date and never wanted to share anything about myself with anyone. I guess I'm just scared of commitment. I mean look at what happened to Bevi, she finally committed and now she's nursing a heartbreak."

Crap, I was getting too heavy there. But to my relief, she responded with her old flair. "I've found relationships to be like that. Kind of why I stay unattached. Though I must say, one night hookups have been getting pretty old lately. Hell, Ballyhoo last night was the first time I'd been on the prowl for weeks."

I realized that we had a lot in common that way.

We just chatted about odds and ends for a few minutes after that. Then I said, "Gotta go, I'm coming up to the exit, be there in ten." I was rewarded with a cute, "Kay, bye!" I smiled out a "Bye," myself as I hung up and descended the exit ramp from I5 into the city center.

I parked a block away in one of those 'sell your kidney' expensive lots and walked up to the old brick building that had been converted into mid-range lofts where she lived. I liked it, it just oozed historic charm. At the curb I saw my first surprise for her waiting patiently. I smiled that direction then went up to the door and buzzed her apartment.

"Who is it? What do you want?! Go away!" I heard her over the intercom, her voice full of humor. I played along, "Ok, I'll just have to go find some other hot girl to date." The door lock buzzed and I went in. I noted the line of mailboxes in the wall in the lobby as I walked along. J. McKay was displayed on box 203. Ahhh, McKay, her last name. I filed it away in my head. Then I walked up the beautifully restored staircase with the cast iron railing to the second floor, instead of taking the pretty cage elevator. I always take stairs when I can, they do wonders for my calves.

There were only three lofts on this level and I walked to the end to 203. The door was slightly ajar. I knocked and head her call out "Come on in, I'm just grabbing my purse!" So I pushed the door open the rest of the way and stepped in.

Wow! Everything about the space resonated charm. From the old brick walls to the cast iron fixtures and inlaid oak. Right down to the worn but well maintained original hardwood floors with the simple throw rugs and runners.

It was one large open space, like a warehouse, with exposed open beams. There were a couple doors on the far end beside the freestanding kitchen space. I assumed those were bedrooms or a bedroom and bathroom. It was sort of messy, but it was a comfortable 'lived in' messy.

"So you think I'm hot?" I heard from the back room.

I looked up as she walked out of one of the doors at the end and she stuttered to a stop when our eyes met, her mouth hanging open. If time hadn't just stopped I'd swear we had both just gasped as my heart stopped. *My God!* She was stunning, no, stunning would be an insult to how spectacular she looked in that maroon dress and heels which matched mine exactly.

It wasn't the grace in which she had walked into the room that held my attention, but her hair that was pulled into a messy bun, held in place by ornate chopsticks, displaying her lusciously long neck just begging for someone's lips to sample the exposed flesh. Her eyes were done up smoky and seductive, and her lips glimmered from across the room. I didn't want to break the moment. Brain to mouth circuitry wasn't fully functional but I managed a single syllable, "Yes."

We snapped out of it and I started twirling the end of my ponytail in my fingers, biting my lower lip. "I mean, you look lovely Riley. Shall we?" I offered an arm which she took, her eyes not leaving mine as she gently took it.

"Umm... you too." she smiled.

We walked toward the stairs and she started to slow down near the elevator but I caught a quick smile play at her lips when she realized I was heading toward the staircase.

I opened the lobby door for her and we stepped out to the sidewalk and she stopped in shock in front of the antique Cinderella style carriage that was hooked up to a beautiful mammoth Clydesdale draft horse. The driver placed a velvet covered step on the curb and offered his hand to Riley.

She delicately grasped it as he helped her in while she took in his formal Victorian attire. Then he similarly helped me up beside her. She had a childlike smile of wonder on her face that made me smile similarly as I spoke after the driver mounted his seat up front.

"Fredrick, this is Jane." I said and turned to her, "Riley, Frederick will be our driver tonight. And that lovely lady up front helping him out is Flower." The horse snorted when I said her name.

Riley nodded toward them both respectively. "Fredrick, Flower, it's nice to meet you." she said sweetly.

Fredrick nodded with a smile mouthing a, "Wow!" to me when Riley was looking away, then he turned toward the front and we started down the road.

We were actually less than four blocks away from our destination, but I had something else in mind. I grabbed Riley's hand and laced our fingers as we trotted down First. She looked excited as we just chatted about nonsensical things, more intent at looking at the city we knew like the back of our hands, pass by from a new perspective.

We turned onto Pike Place and rode past the market, watching the vendors packing up for the day. It was a nice leisurely pace, then we cut down to Alaska Way and circled back past the ferry docks and the aquarium, stopping for a moment by that awesome Mia Jacobs hubcap mural. Then we continued on until we got to King street and stopped at a restored six story brick building.

She gasped, "Alessandro's? There's a six month waiting list here!"

I smiled and winked at this. "I'm owed a favor."

I swear I heard Fredrick snort, cheeky boy, or was it Flower? Frederick ran around and placed the step and helped us down and asked me quietly, "So are we even now?"

I shook my head and whispered back, "If only." We shared a smile. I noticed Riley caught the exchange as the carriage trotted off.

"Another owed favor?" she asked, cocking one of those perfectly sculpted eyebrows at me in mirth.

I started fidgeting with the end of my ponytail and laughed nervously. "Something like that." We walked into the building and to the elevator this time since Alessandro's Italian Restaurant occupied the top floor.

Once the doors opened, the stunningly handsome Italian man who was standing over by the maitre'd glanced over and smiled hugely then hustled to us. Offering an arm to each of us as he spoke brightly in a thick Italian accent, "Miss James! We've been expecting you. And..."

I interjected as he left the question implied, " Alessandro, this is Jane. Miss Jane McKay. And how many times do I have to tell you to please call me Crystal?"

"Miss McKay, it is a pleasure. This is the first time Crystal has ever brought someone other than her sister, Beverly here. This is exciting!"

I shot a look at him telling him he was sharing too much. He caught on and clammed up as he lead us through the restaurant.

Riley responded, "No, the pleasure is mine." I caught Riley giving me an odd reappraising look with a smile.

She looked a little confused as we were led out of the dining area and into the kitchen. I whispered to Alessandro, "Is everything set up?"

He responded as he led us to the fire exit door, "Just as requested."

I caught her raised eyebrow. *Damnit, she's got ears like a bat*! But I simply love watching that eyebrow.

We went out the fire door and up the stairs to the door marked 'Roof Access' and he pushed it open. Riley gasped. A purple runner ran out to a single table on a huge purple area rug near the roof parapet, where a single table lit by candles sat with two meals covered by silver domes. The sun was dipping into Puget Sound, throwing reds and oranges across the cloudy sky. There were Birds of Paradise flowers arranged in large standing floor vases on each corner of the rug, pinning it down.

Alessandro walked us out and held our chairs as we sat, then took each of our hands giving them a kiss. "Have a wonderful evening ladies." He wandered back downstairs as soft music started playing from hidden speakers somewhere.

Riley's eyes were darting around, taking everything in. "The rug... purple, my favorite color. And Birds of Paradise? Italian food? I barely mentioned these things last night. You remembered it all?" She seemed flustered.

I smiled and replied, "Not a thing you've said to me that I don't remember."

"How did you get these things on such short notice?" she suddenly asked. I started to answer "Some people owed..." But she cut me off, "Owed you a favor?" We shared a laugh as I nodded sheepishly.

We took the lids off the meals and I poured the champagne. The easy conversation that flowed between us as we ate was as easy as speaking with Bev. Like we had been doing it our whole lives.

It was finally dusk, I glanced at my cellphone for the time. 8:58pm. I put my napkin on my plate then stood and reached my hand out to her. She took it, a questioning look on her face. I brought her a couple steps from the table and brought her in close to me and started slowly dancing to the music.

She happily surrendered as we melted into each other easily, swaying to the music. I glanced at the football stadium that dominated the view just as the first of the fireworks were launched into the sky exactly like I knew they would since the exhibition game there was slated to start at 9:00pm. I pulled back from her but continued to dance and held her hands in mine.

I watched as her eyes twinkled, mirroring the display in the sky. Then I couldn't stop myself, I had been watching her lips all night. I leaned in and softly captured her lips with mine.

It was a soft, probing kiss that she returned with more passion. I traced her lower lip with my tongue as she did the same. Every cell in my body felt flush with heat as she parted her lips slightly and our tongues gently caressed each others.

Then the first raindrop fell on us to interrupt our evening. We broke the kiss, both of us gasping and looking to the sky, her eyes were glazed over like I'm sure mine were. We smiled hugely to each other then laughed and sprinted toward the door to avoid the rain.

We just made it into the stairwell when the clouds opened up. Alessandro and two busboys were already on their way up to get everything out of the rain.

He stopped as we reached each other. "I'm so sorry your night has been ruined. But this is Seattle, rain is rain."

I smiled at him and assured him, "No, everything was perfect." I cringed at the dreamy tone in my voice on the word perfect. "However, I was planning a leisurely stroll back to your place to finish the night, Riley." I shrugged a sheepish apology even though I didn't mind the rain myself.

She was grinning, I could tell she was having a good time despite the rain when she spoke, "No it's fine. I simply love the rain. Why else would I choose to live in Seattle? I'd still like that walk."

Alessandro raised a finger and darted into the kitchen before us and returned handing me an umbrella before we made our way into the restaurant. I excused myself as we passed the restroom and they stood by the door to wait. Like an idiot I hadn't gone since after lunch, I was too nervous getting ready.

I quickly did my thing and washed my hands; but as I was about to open the door, I heard Riley and Alessandro speaking. She was asking him about the 'favor' I called in to get us there. He explained to her that with all the parties I arrange everywhere, I charge my fee up front to my clients but *NEVER* take a commission from any of the vendors I use, like his restaurant. Instead of currency, I liked to trade in favors, making things very beneficial to all involved.

I blushed when I heard him say, "She is extremely liked and respected in the local entertainment and hospitality industries in Seattle because of it. I'm pleased to count her as one of my friends."

I waited a few seconds then opened the door and smiled at Riley, "Ready?" She smiled hugely back and nodded. I swear her eyes were twinkling at me.

Alessandro kissed the back of each of our hands as we said our goodbyes to him and boarded the elevator. As we rode down her hand snaked out and grabbed mine. Lacing our fingers together.

We walked out into the lobby and approached the door. I released her hand and opened the umbrella as we walked outside before seeking the warmth of her grasp again. We walked in a comfortable silence for a block stealing lingering glances at each other.

I looked around at the city as we walked. Seeing the rain in the streetlamps, the ground reflecting the lights in the gathering pools. I loved the rain, it made the city look new. It felt like it washed away anything that tainted it. Brought life to things.

Washed away any hidden guilt from your soul. I stopped and handed Riley the umbrella and started taking off my heels and dropping my purse.

"What are you doing?" she laughed out.

I walked away from the shelter of the umbrella. I smiled innocently at her as I took a few steps and looked to the sky and started turning slowly, holding my arms out to my side. Letting the rain wash over me to wash away my sins. I opened my mouth in a genuine smile and spun around, still staring at the sky.

"God, this feels good!" I said wistfully, "It's like the whole world is brand new when it rains!" I finally stopped turning and jumped onto the base of an old fashioned streetlight, smiling hugely at her and pushing the loose straggles of wet hair from my eyes. Basking in the feeling.

"Wow." she said, with eyes full of wonder and biting her lower lip hungrily as she continued, "You look so... innocent. Happy."

I ran back under the umbrella grabbing my discarded items, slipping my shoes back on and hugging her arm and not letting go as I started pulling her toward her loft. I'm sure my eyes were twinkling, "I *AM* happy!"

At the door, she unlocked it as I stood on the sidewalk, she turned back for a second and I took a step to her and kissed her passionately. When we broke it off, I gasped out, "Good night Riley."

She shook her head slowly, her smile turning to a look of sadness, "Good night Cryster. Sometimes I forget this is just a game."

Then she walked into the building before I could respond. *Yeah. A game. I forgot that's all it is to her.* I wandered off toward my car, confused about the night.

Chapter 5 – Second Date

I got home, still soaked to the bone a half an hour later and confused as hell. I walked in the door and felt like crying and I had absolutely no clue why. Bev looked back at me from the couch where she was watching a movie. Then without a word she stood and ran to my bedroom, coming out with a oversized t-shirt, a towel and my heavy robe.

I saw her concern, but I didn't know what to say, I was cycling through emotions. So I just stood there like a helpless idiot as she undressed me, patted me down with the towel and put me into my night clothes. Then she led me to the couch like a child and started drying my hair with the towel as she just held me. She still hadn't said a word and I just silently cried into her shoulder.

Time marched on, then it was midnight. I was still hiding in her protective arms when I sniffed. "Thanks Bevi, I don't know what the hell was wrong with me."

She smiled at me then quietly said, "You like her, Kru."

I don't know if it was a question or a statement as I replied, "No... yes... maybe... God, I don't know. It was like the perfect Cinderella date and, I don't know, maybe I was getting way too into it. But then she reminded me that it was just a game, a stupid bet. I guess I needed to be reminded of that. That she wasn't feeling the same confusion as me."

Bev looked at me with her "I don't think so sis." look but didn't say anything. The phone in my purse on the floor started buzzing. She got up and grabbed it then looked at the screen and handed it to me. A text from Riley. I took a cleansing breath then read it. *[thx 4 the most amazing time 2nite. srry 4 ruining it at end. :( ]*

I didn't know how to take it, maybe she *WAS* feeling something, or maybe I'm just reading too much into it. I texted back quickly with an ambiguous *[no worries. had amazing time w/ u. can't wait til 2morow :)]*. And seconds later I got her response. *[whew. thought i messed up. can i ask, what did 2nite set you back? research 4 2morrow date]*. I smiled as I shot back, *[the price of ur dress, a 12 pack of beer, and calling in a few markers]*. I was quite proud of myself for what I pulled off on a shoestring budget.

A *[u looked awesome 2nite. g'night cryster]* came back a second later that made my heart flutter. I typed back, *[u looked spectacular too. g'night riley]*. I was beaming as I looked over at Bev who was reading the entire exchange.

She looked at me grinning, "Oh my God! My best friend *IS*

gay!"

I smiled at her and meekly replied, "Starting to look that way." But then I lost my smile. "Too bad it's just a game to her."

She placed a hand on my shoulder and said with concern in her voice, "You need to put a stop to this before you really get hurt. Think tonight times ten, Kru."

I shrugged and attempted to assure her, "It's just one more date."

I tried to hide the fact that I just wanted as much time as I could with Riley before this bet was over and she moved on. But the squinty look Bev was shooting me told me she wasn't buying my BS.

She shook her head then stood again looking between our bedrooms then asked, "Snuggle time or no?"

I just nodded, I was still a little emotionally raw so we made our way into my bedroom and snuggled into bed, cocooning ourselves in, protecting each other from the stresses of our two bizzaroland broken relationships.

- - -

I awoke to sun streaming in the window and the sound of Bev in the shower and my phone buzzing on the nightstand. I looked at the time on it, 8:01am, before looking at the text message. Oooh! It's from her! *[mornin sleepyhead. i b there at 9. dress casual and light jacket]* I wanted to run around in little circles. I shot back an *[already ready]*. *Lies! Lies I say!* Just an hour! I had to get ready. It was a daytime date! She never said anything!

I ran to the shower and was simultaneously stripping and grabbing a slippery wet Bev from around the shower curtain and pulling her out of the shower so I could take mine.

"Hey! Pushy much, sis?" I got playfully from her as I stepped in. Her hand rocketed back into the shower to turn off the hot water before running off laughing maniacally at the "Jesus!" I screamed at the cold water hitting my body.

I finished my shower and stepped out yelling, "Bevi!" As I dried off and put on some clean undergarments, then stared into my closet. She came walking in wearing just her bra and panties, finishing up eating a bowl of my Fruit Loops.

"Yeashh?" she said, nonchalantly with her mouth full of those heavenly sugary loops.

"What the hell does casual mean? Is that like, here's my running sweats casual? I'm just hangin' at the mall casual? I'm really dressing sexier than hell but kicking it like it's casual, casual?" I blurted in a panic.

She snorted. *Yes, she actually snorted at my distress! What kind of friend does that? I'm so going to demote her from best friend status! I mean, well there's nobody else to promote, so I guess she stays, but she is so on my list! If I had a list that is!*

She was waving her spoon in front of my face to get my attention and asked me with her lopsided grin, "Internal friend demotion rant?"

I nodded with a smirk as she rummaged around in my drawers and pulled out my regular every day clothes. Some low rise jeans, my favorite solid red tank tee. My converse and some white socks. She included my white mini pants, just in case a swimming emergency arises.

"Taaa daa!" she offered.

She's a genius! Never in a million years would I have... oh... wait... duh, that's what I always wear. I decided that I really had to relax. The evil redhead could read all this in my expression and rolled her eyes as she wandered back out of my room munching my cereal, calling back over her shoulder with a giggle, "You're so friggin' gay for her!"

I pulled my hair into its signature ponytail, making sure to have some stragglers loose across my face as the door intercom buzzed. I ran over to the door but walked the last few steps after hearing Bev cracking up over on the couch about it while eating another full bowl of my Fruit Loops.

I hit the intercom, "Sorry, we already donated." I said smirking. Then I heard Riley repeat my own words back to me.

"Ok, I'll just have to go find some other hot girl to date." I snorted and hit the door buzzer then opened our door a crack and wandered into my bedroom to grab my purse and a light white hooded jacket.

I heard the gentle knock on the front door and heard Bev, "Come on in. Sup Jane?"

Riley responded, "Hi, Beverly, is Crystal ready?"

Bevi replied, "Yeah, little miss 'freak out' is getting her purse. Fruit Loops?"

Riley laughed, "No, but thanks. You aren't wearing any

clothes, Bev."

To her comedic, no-modesty credit, my best friend answered, "Huh. How bout that?"

I saw her shrug as she shoveled another spoonful of sugary goodness into her mouth as I walked out into the living room.

"Hey." I said as I walked up to Riley. She was wearing an almost identical outfit, her top was pink and white stripped though. She turned and a big smile grew on her face. I couldn't have stopped my own return smile even if I had tried... which I didn't.

"Hey back." she said. "Ready to hit the road?"

She nodded a goodbye to Bev and I followed her out. I caught Bevi mouthing, "Be careful." to me as I closed the door.

Riley said, "She wasn't wearing any clothes," to me as we walked out toward her car.

Was that a tinge of jealousy in her voice? Couldn't be. "Huh. How bout that?" I parroted Bev's earlier statement. Then a second later grinned at Riley and said, "Yeah, she's not real big on the whole 'modesty' myth."

She almost laughed at that, "Myth?"

I chuckled and said, "Yeah, according to Bevi."

She seemed amused now but still asked, "She do that sort of thing often?"

Oh, I got it now. "Why? You like?"

She shook her head. "No, like I said before, not interested in *HER*."

Ok, now it sounded like jealousy again as well as some flirting. Mixed signals much? I blushed and responded, "Well, nothing to worry about, that's just how she is. She's my best friend who may as well be my sister."

She defended herself quickly, "I'm not worried. She's just so easygoing about it. Besides, we're not really dating."

That stung and she saw me flinch and quickly added, "Sorry, didn't mean it like that. I didn't mean to ruin the date before it starts." Her shoulders slumped.

She looked dejected, I just wanted to hold her, so I

compromised and grabbed her hand as we walked, slipping my fingers between hers. Then reassured her by simply saying softly, "Nothing is ruined." I caught her smile out of the corner of my eye, causing my own to reappear.

We hopped in her car and she was really secretive as we looped into Seattle then drove back out of the city on I90, I couldn't dig any details out of her so I settled on smalltalk and joking around with her. We slipped into our easy banter again. Learning all we could about each other. It was so easy, so natural.

We turned off at Issaquah and darted under the interstate to a private airfield. *OMG are we going to fly?* She nodded to the guard at the gate who just smiled and waved us in. She parked next to a hangar that she said she shared with multiple pilots and got out and ran around to get my door. I grinned and blushed at that, nervously twirling the end of my ponytail.

She typed a code on a pad at the huge bay door and the machinery groaned as the door rolled aside, revealing a few small planes. Up front was her gleaming white plane with purple wingtips and leading edges. There was an awesome, brilliant purple wavy stripe along the body with 'McKay Air Tours' painted inside the stripe in white. She walked up to it, running her fingers along it and beaming with pride.

"Wow!" I said, "It's beautiful!"

She grinned like an idiot and replied, "She's my baby. Cryster, meet Violet."

She grabbed my hand and excitedly dragged me into the shared walled off office area inside the hangar. "Wait here a minute, I gotta go do pre-flight." she grinned.

I smiled while biting my lower lip as I watched her run out toward her plane through the huge windows lining the wall. She was almost bounding like a little kid, it brought another smile to my face to watch her enthusiasm.

I noticed music coming from a small radio near an old orange vinyl couch that must have come from the 1970's. I walked over to sit and wait. The only modern thing in office area was a print of one of those trippily cool collages by Mia Jacobs.

I saw some magazines on the old 1970's looking coffee table with its fake wood melamine surface. When I looked at them, I actually laughed out loud. They were four 'HotRod' magazines dated from more than a decade ago.

Just then, 4Ever by The Veronicas came on the radio. *I friggin' love this song!* I reached over to the radio and cranked it then stood then started bouncing and dancing, gyrating my hips and banging my head as I sang along with one arm in the air, flexing my wrist with a finger outstretched to the beat.

The song ended and I reached down to the radio and lowered the volume again. The color drained from my face when I heard someone clapping slowly from the door. I turned to see Riley with a hungry look in her eyes. *Was that lust?*

She said to me in a husky voice, her eyes darker than normal, "Admit it, you were just sent from the heavens as a cruel joke to torture me. That was just... wow... but you're friggin' straight! Not even remotely fair."

"Feelin' kind of bendy lately," I said to myself under my breath. Her perfectly sculpted eyebrow arched again. *Damn her and her bat-like hearing!*

She grinned and held her hand out for me to take. "Come on! Time to fly!"

I walked over and bashfully took her hand, feeling a fire spread from where her soft skin touched mine. She turned and dragged me out to Violet, helping me into the copilot seat. Then she ran around and hopped up into the pilot's seat and grinned at me.

"Ok, put this on so you can hear my conversation with the tower. I'll be VOX but they can't hear you unless you hit the PTT button on the cable. You won't ever need to." She handed me a headset and put one on herself. Then she pulled out an iPad and went through her checklist and pulled up a GPS map while flipping switches and messing with the controls.

I saw the yoke in front of me move as she tested her's. She caught my look and said with a smile, "You don't want to be touching that when we're in the air." She winked.

I started nervously playing with the end of my ponytail and chewing on my lower lip. Then the propeller started spinning as Violet roared to life, the excited smile that grew on Riley's face and the joy twinkling in her eyes told me the story of her love for flying. The engine wasn't as loud as I thought it would be as Violet growled low, like a caged beast.

We taxied out of the hangar and stopped, then Riley spoke with the tower, requesting taxi to the runway and flight clearance. After we receiving a taxi go ahead, we trundled out and turned to the end of the runway. The tower gave clearance. She glanced to me then grasped the throttle control with a look of glee, and the sound level doubled as we suddenly shot down the runway.

I was pulling on my ponytail now, then Riley looked over to me with a huge smile and wink, pulling back on the yoke. My stomach fell as we escaped gravity, we were flying! It was exhilarating, it felt just like I felt whenever I got lost in Riley's eyes.

I've flown dozens of times on commercial jets, but that was nothing compared to the feeling of freedom that I was experiencing now. I shot an excited smile over to Riley who had not stopped smiling since we boarded Violet. My heart was racing.

We circled the field once then headed east into the Cascades with her deftly handling the controls, the plane slicing through the air like we were riding on glass.

She switched channels on the radio and called out, "Silent Bob, this is Jane, do you read?"

A moment later an extremely female voice replied, not what I would have expected from a Bob. "I read you Jane, everything is ready. Kim just got back."

She smiled and replied, "Thank you Bobbi, catch you on the flip side." Then she switched channels back.

I found the call sign amusing. Geek much Riley?

"What was that about?" I spoke loudly over the engine.

She smirked as she cryptically replied, "Just calling in a favor."

I rolled my eyes at her amusement at throwing that in my face. "Funny." I mocked. *But it was funny.*

She shrugged and simply said, "Put your hands on the yoke."

I looked at her like she had just asked me to kiss a rattlesnake. Which honestly, I probably would do for her, if she asked.

She smiled at my expression and said, "Don't worry. Put your hands on the yoke."

I did and she started a series of gentle banks, then gained some altitude and dove gently before leveling out again. I could feel everything she did smooth and gentle. She was doing something with her feet a little too, I could see the pedals by my feet moving a bit.

Smiling, she echoed what I felt. "Smooth and gentle movements, like making love. No quick or extreme moves. Now you try, I'll handle the pedals." She smiled encouragingly to me as she raised her hands about a half inch from the controls, at the ready.

I slowly started a bank. *Oh my god! This is awesome!* I'm sure my smile was threatening to split my face in half. I banked the other direction. Then I tried to raise altitude a little and did a gentle dive and leveled out just like she showed me.

I couldn't have wiped the excited smile off my face if you had paid me to. She smiled back at me and took the controls again. I took my hands off the yoke and gushed at her, my heart beating fast, "That was so amazing!" Her eyes were twinkling at me as she breathed out, "I know right?" Then she smoothly broke us into a steep diving bank. Inserting us neatly into a valley between two rocky peaks.

We swooped down between two beautiful tree lined ridges and we loitered in the area, passing a tiny lake and beautiful waterfall feeding it. Then we circled back around and she lined us up with a little clearing in the middle of the forest with a dirt runway lined that was with bright orange wind socks.

We landed smooth as silk, the only roughness came from the uneven ground beneath the wheels. We slowed and she taxied us into the grass field beside the strip then cut the engine. My heart was still beating fast from the exhilaration. I bit my lower lip and played with my ponytail as I stared at her.

Riley grinned and took off her headset, I followed suit. "So what do you think so far?" she asked with a confident grin. I just nodded like an idiot, not speaking.

She laughed and opened her door and jumped down then ran around Violet to my door and opened it, helping me down.

My legs were a little wobbly and I exclaimed, "Whoa, it feels like we are still flying!"

She laughed in understanding, "Yeah it'll pass in a minute. Come on!"

It was slightly nippy and we both put on our light jackets we had tied at our waists. Then she grabbed my hand and our fingers just naturally found their way between each others.

She started dragging me off into the woods. "This is an old ranger's strip. They still use it from time to time," she said as we went deeper on a trail into the forest.

A minute later we popped out into a clearing by that large waterfall we had seen from the air. I gasped and she smiled at my reaction as she pulled me a little further. I was still stunned by the beauty of nature when I felt her pulling me down onto the ground.

I looked down as we sat, I didn't even notice we had come up to a red checkered blanket with an old fashioned picnic basket. *Where did this come from? Oh, Silent Bob!*

Riley laughed a little as she read my thought process through my expressions. Only Bev had mastered that feat.

"This was all just my way to get you alone for lunch." She smiled at her ingenuity. I just smiled at *HER*.

We dug the simple food and soft drinks out of the basket and placed them on the blanket. She slid behind me, with me sitting between her legs, leaning back to rest against her. *I could sit like this forever.* And we started eating. I grabbed one of the sandwiches and tentatively peeked under the top slice of bread.

Tuna sandwich! But eww... sliced pickles on it. I started to take the pickles off, but when she smiled oddly at me, I squinted at her then licked one timidly. *Oh! Sweet pickles! OMG she remembered!* The pickle went back in place and I happily munched on the sandwich. "You remembered." I gushed.

She threw my own words back at me once again with a soft,

caring smile, "Not a thing you've said to me that I don't remember." I melted. She was perfect.

We talked and joked through lunch, taking in the nature around us. I felt so at ease and I hoped she did too. We laid down on the blanket for a while as topics got deeper. Our eyes never left each others. She mentioned again that she loved my dual tone eyes, that she could live in them forever. I wound up snuggled into her with my back to her front, her arm draped across my waist as we discussed our hopes and dreams.

I cocked my head back to look up at her wonderfully smiling face and stretched up a bit for a soft quick kiss. We both sighed. Then it was time to go, far too soon for me. We packed everything including the blanket into the the picnic basket and made our way slowly back to the plane.

With everything stowed she helped me in, stopping for a gentle kiss first. Then we were airborne again. Winging ourselves west, back to Issaquah, I even got to fly again!

It was a comfortable silence until we landed and taxied back into the hangar. I was staring at Riley, memorizing every curve of her face, of her lips, and whispered before we got out, "I don't want this date to end."

She helped me down then put her lips beside my ear, her hot breath on my neck doing marvelous things to me. "Who said it was over? That... was just lunch. I wanted to share some of my private world with you like you shared yours," she whispered.

She could have taken me right there on the hangar floor and I would have willingly given myself to her. *I don't have any question in my head anymore. Bev was right. I am sooo gay for this girl.*

She locked up the hangar then I walked jelly legged to the car. She opened the door for me and then got in the drivers seat and we were off, darting under the freeway again but not getting on it. Instead she brought us past Gilman Village and up the little mountain behind it.

At the top we pulled into a zoo parking lot. There was a friggin zoo here in Issaquah and I never knew about it! Cougar Mountain Zoological Park. I've lived in this area my entire life and a zoo has been hiding here the whole time? The signs indicate it is a teaching zoo. I looked at her, "I had no clue this was here Riley."

She grinned. "Most people don't. Come on!"

We went inside the main building and into an admin area.

Were we supposed to be here? We walked toward a back office, a couple people nodded at Riley.

"What are we doing here?" I whispered.

She winked at me with confidence, her charisma oozing from her pores, "Just calling in a marker."

We reached the back office and she knocked lightly and a moment later a cute, smiling Asian girl about our age opened the door.

"Jane!" She exclaimed. Then the girl looked at me. "Whoa! You weren't kidding. Hot! And those eyes, yum!"

I was blushing as Riley slapped her arm. "Hey! Eyes off lady, she's with me. Tak, this is Crystal. Cryster this is Takara." I shook her hand.

Then Riley continued, "So what 'learning experience' you got lined up for us Tak?"

The girl just smiled and motioned for us to follow her. We went out a side door and into a utility cart and down path at the backside of the zoo.

She brought us to a double gate and Riley just said, "Sweet! You are going to love this, Cryster!" We went inside the first gate and we were each handed a feed bucket by the guy doing some maintenance there, and Takara opened the second gate and spoke to me with a soft smile, "Jane knows all the rules, just follow her lead. I'll be out here when you guys are done."

I was confused but Riley grabbed my free hand with hers and pulled me deeper into the enclosure. We turned a corner and I almost dropped my bucket. Little reindeer! There were a bunch of little reindeer in front of me grazing! I glanced at Riley and she was just watching the excitement on my face. Her own smile was threatening to split her face wide open.

She moved slowly, then when we were noticed, a group of them basically surrounded us and were trying to stick their noses in our buckets. "Do what I do," she said and started grabbing handfuls of the feed out of the bucket and offering it to them, they ate out of her hand.

I smiled again and did the same. *This is me. Standing here. Feeding rein-freaking-deer!* They were amazing and so furry, a lot furrier than I could have imagined. I was so excited!

Riley reached out and stroked an antler. "Feel them."

I mimicked her, I was surprised that they were soft and covered with a velvet like fuzz.

Then she started throwing handfuls of feed around on the ground. I followed suit. Finally she upended her bucket for one to put his nose in to see it was empty. Then we wandered back to Takara. I kept looking back and was mouthing, "Wow, wow, wow," while the two girls laughed at me.

Then we said our goodbyes and left Tak and went into the zoo proper to do the touristy thing and look at all the cool animals everywhere. It was a small zoo but I didn't care. *Did I mention I fed reindeer!?* We went everywhere holding hands, our fingers constantly laced. It was a comfortable afternoon as we chatted and laughed.

I was sad when we returned to the car for the trip home. Riley smiled. "So it seems you aren't the only one with contacts." She waggled her perfect eyebrows.

I was suddenly a little unsettled thinking about Takara and Silent Bob. "Old girlfriends?"

Riley quickly said, "I plea the fifth."

I looked down at my hands and she quickly added, "It was a

long time ago, we're just friends now." *I don't like this feeling. Am I jealous?*

"It's fine." I said quietly. *Come on me don't ruin this fun day.*

I forced myself to brighten. "Thanks for such an amazing day! This is going on my top one list." This got her smile to return. I could live in her smile. We cranked the radio and sang at the top of our lungs the whole way back as I danced in my seat.

We pulled into the parking lot as 'Hangover' by Hey Monday came on. I stopped her from turning the car off, placing my hand on hers as she reached for the key. "Wait!" I jumped out of the car and started dancing right there in the parking lot, singing the chorus and swinging my hips and bobbing.

Riley had a silly grin on her face, just watching me have fun. The song was mostly over when the words were sinking in for me... they were hitting way too close to home just now. I stopped and reached in and shut off the radio. Riley looked concerned and shut off the car and got out to stand beside me.

I shrugged it off and grabbed my ponytail then shot her my most innocent smile. She looked relieved and... ummm... aroused? This affected me in a similar manner. *Holy crap.*

She walked me to the door and I turned to her and looked down shyly. "I had a really great time Riley. Thank you."

She leaned in, our lips brushed and I was in heaven again. Our hands meeting and our fingers lacing on their own. It was so sweet, sensual, sexy and fun, all at the same time. Like every kiss should be. I was lost, trying to feed her my passion as I received hers. We broke it off so that we could gasp for air.

"Good night Cryster." she whispered.

She turned to leave but I didn't release her hands. "Don't go," I whispered. "Come up and have dinner with Bev and I. I'd love to visit with you some more."

She nodded and I dropped one hand to get my keys and soon we were walking into the living room upstairs with Bevi dancing and singing to the Mandy Fay Harris Farewell Tour on TV... still in her underwear. We both laughed and she spun around smiling at us.

"Hi guys!" she said excitedly then she ran over and put us into a group hug.

"Umm... Beverly. Clothes?" Riley squeaked.

Bev looked down at herself. "Oh. Gothcha!" She wandered into her room to find something to wear. She came back out a second later wearing just a worn out band t-shirt and we all sat on the couch and called for pizza delivery.

We all chatted casually until the pizza delivery guy was buzzed in. I walked to the kitchen counter for my purse but Bev beat me to it. Riley and I couldn't contain our laughter until the door was closed over his shock at a sexy redhead paying in nothing but a t-shirt. He gave her almost a full book of discount coupons as he tried to regain the ability to speak.

The oblivious redhead wandered over to the couch with the pizza with a questioning look on her face. Riley spoke up cheerfully, "You really don't have any shame do you, Bev?"

Bev replied, "Huh?"

Looking to me for explanation. I glanced dramatically down at her clothing choice and it dawned on her. "Oh that. I got us some coupons!" she responded enthusiastically. We all shared a laugh as we grabbed some slices.

"So spill chicks!" Bev looked at us expectantly. "Who gives better date?" *Riley wins hands down!* I mouthed with my eyes wide, "Riley. OMG!" to Bevi when Riley's was leaning forward to grab a napkin off the coffee table.

Then I spoke up coyly, "Well, I'm not sure. It seems too close for me to call. I mean yeah, she had some jaw dropping things up her sleeve and it was amazingly fun. But I pulled out all the romance stops."

Riley looked dejected and I'm not sure why. She said, "I keep forgetting this is just a game."

Now it was my turn to look dejected. She continued, "Yeah, Cryster knew every button to push to make a girl swoon. But I stepped things up a notch in the *FUN* department with my play. I'd say it was too close to call."

This gave me hope, maybe I can spin this so I can spend more time with her. It is obvious she only sees this as a bet.

"So, with no clear winner. Then I guess we move to round two." I announced.

Riley suddenly looked happier. "Oh yes! By all means. Prepare to go down, Cryster."

I absentmindedly joked, "If you want, it will be our third date after all." My hands slapped over my mouth, my pizza flinging behind me onto the floor. I could have died right there. *I had no intention of saying that out loud!*

Riley was staring at me in shock. I wanted to run and hide, but Bev came to the rescue and broke the awkwardness chuckling, "Hey wait a second! Now that I think about it... I've *NEVER* seen you make it to a third date, Kru. Holy crap! This will be the longest relationship you have ever had. And I've known you for..." she pretended to count on her fingers, "...forever! You must be magic, Jane!"

Riley looked at her then at me, while I was still trying to figure out how to die from my earlier embarrassment. The she asked, "You were serious when you told me you never made it past a second date?" She was smiling; but then I saw the light suddenly go out in her sparkling eyes as she continued, "Only it's just pretend now."

Damnit! I wish it meant as much to her as it did me. "I guess." I said sadly. Then tried to brighten, "So, when's your next day off? I got a party to plan this week and some work on iFORk. I'll be busy Tuesday through Thursday. Or Wednesday if I pull in a favor or two since I know a guy with a camel for the iFORk. Hard to find many animals this year, but I located a few. But my nights are always free." The girls each quirked an eyebrow at 'camel'. I snorted.

Curiosity tinged Riley's voice. "What's iFORk and why do they need a camel?"

Before I could speak Bev stepped up. "It's the annual iFORk Children's Festival. It simply stands for 'It's For Kids'. They do it in a different month every year."

Riley nodded, realization on her face. "Oh yeah, that citywide party for children from low income families."

Bevi puffed her chest up with pride as she spoke, as I tried to hide. "That's Kru's baby. It was her Marketing 101 freshman project seven years back. Trying to see if she could organize a citywide event on a zero budget by getting all the vendors involved to donate time and materials for the publicity alone. Not a penny crossed anyone's palms. She called in a few markers, she was networking even back then. And she frigging did it!"

"How the hell does an eighteen year old girl pull off a pirate themed party with twenty thousand people in attendance and have a real frigging pirate ship there? She somehow got the 'Amazing Grace' to sail across Puget Sound from Gig Harbor, and up the Ballard Locks into Lake Union with a pirate flag, to the Wooden Boat Museum downtown for the kids to tour! She got a damn tall ship!" She shook her head and Riley was smiling with wide sparkling eyes.

I shrugged in embarrassment. "Well I knew the captain, he..." Riley interrupted "...owed you a favor." I lowered my eyes as the two girl's laughed.

Bev continued, "And from what I hear, the captain *STILL* owes her a favor! Well that led to her current job and her web of contacts has grown exponentially since. Hell, this condo we got for a steal. She 'knew a guy'. This year's iFORk theme is 'Urban Safari' so I'm guessing that's where the camel comes in."

Riley was just looking at me with amazement on her face, and something... else? Then her face brightened. "Hang on a second," she said holding up a finger, then fished her phone out and hit a speed dial.

"Hi Tak, yeah it's me Jane. No. Yeah, she is isn't she? No I'm still with her here, keep your eyes off her. Well, you guys still do those educational outings with some of the animals? Yeah? You hear of the iFORk? Yeah, that *WOULD* be great publicity for Cougar Mountain... well, no. Yeah. What if I could hook you up there? You won't believe this but Crystal *IS* iFORk! No, I'm not shitting you. Yeah, I'll have her contact you. You owe me big. No, we were even today with the feeding. Remember me getting Silent Bob to arrange the zoo's winter outing? Thought so. K, gotta go. Bye."

She hung up grinning at me, with me staring at her blankly, then she said, "So think your safari could use some more animals and educational materials, and maybe a reindeer?"

I couldn't help myself but I leaned over and kissed her quickly. I smiled at her shock again. "You really are something Riley." *Did she just blush?*

Then Riley joked back, "You're not the only one with contacts." I bit my lower lip and twirled my ponytail end more intently. Bevi cleared her throat.

"If you two are going to start dry humping here on the couch, just let me know, I'll need popcorn." We both blushed and Riley tried to get us back on topic.

"I've got a really fluid schedule. Only two booked charters on Tuesday and Wednesday, but I'm on retainer for a few local companies. So I'm kinda' on call." Riley offered.

I nodded, then rapid fired out, "So, Monday then? Or is that too soon? That's too soon right? Would that seem needy? I don't want to seem needy. Friday works if Monday is bad. I got some ideas from your date. I could..." Riley was shutting me up again.

I happily allowed her to shut me up like this as I savored the feel of our lips sliding together.

Bevi was clearing her throat again, fanning her face, and we pulled apart gasping. Riley looked over at her with a sheepish smile. "Only way to shut her up sometimes."

I just smiled and nodded enthusiastically, affirming the assertion in a cute tiny voice, "It's true."

Bev squinted at the two of us blushing. "You two sure you're not a couple? You got me convinced."

I was still tingly, I absently laid back into Riley on the couch and started playing with my ponytail. She lazily draped an arm across me as we both denied it. I felt some lips by my ear. "It's whenever you want, just call. But I demand to be wooed." she said. The vibration of her voice on my exposed skin was doing naughty things to me.

"Ok." I squeaked out shyly, lowering my eyes as I bit my lip.

Beverly laughed. "Guess we know who the boss is between you two." *Yes, please.*

I mocked indignation, "She wishes."

After another hour of banter, laughing and sharing, Riley had to say goodnight. We stood and I walked her to the door and held it open. She called over to Bev, "G'night Beverly. It was fun." A hand rose up from the couch waving. I looked shyly at Riley then captured her lips gently with mine, giving her hand a squeeze as I broke the kiss. "G'night Riley."

She was blushing. "G'night, Cryster," she said as she left.

I shut the door and leaned on it with my back to it and exhaled. Then got knocked out of my dreaming by Bevi shouting, "What the hell is wrong with you?"

I lowered my eyes and made my way back to the couch, collapsing on her. "I don't know."

She eyeballed me and voiced, "You're setting yourself up for a big hurt here."

I sighed out, "I know."

Chapter 6 – Sunday Funday

The next morning when sun came streaming into the living room window, hitting us in the face. I slid off the couch being sure to bump Bev as much as I could when I was untangling from her. If I gotta be up this early, I'm sure as heck not going to suffer alone. She groaned and I feigned, "Sorry Bevi, did I wake you?"

She threw a throw pillow at me (Huh, is that why they are called that?) and moaned, "You are so mean," as she stood groggily and wandered toward her room as I went toward mine.

I showered and prepped for a lazy day of lounging around and relaxing. My mind on Riley. Spookily, right on cue my cell buzzed over on my dresser where I put it on the charger earlier. I looked at the screen and laughed out loud, it was from Riley. *[bored]* I quickly replied. *[call me]* Moments later the phone was ringing.

To be a smart ass, I answered again with, "Hey girl! Why you so bored?" Which got her laughing uncontrollably.

Then she said, "Sunday... you got church or something?"

I giggled, "I'd probably burst into flame if I ever entered a church."

She snorted, "Oooo Crispy Cryster! But seriously, that would probably be my fate too. Soooo... talk to me... boredom does not sit well with me."

I smiled as I could picture her 'tortured' self lazily draped across a chair staring at the ceiling on the phone with me. "Brunch?" I stated simply.

"Mmmm... be there in thirty." she said and hung up. I laughed to myself. *Just how cute is she?*

I suddenly felt under dressed in my lounge around the house clothes. Just then Bev poked her head in with a mopey look and said, "I'll be back in a few hours, heading over to Lori's to get my stuff before she throws it out."

I was concerned. "Sure you don't want me to come to kick her cheating butt for you?"

She fought off a smile. "Nah. I got this." Then she narrowed her eyes in suspicion, "You seem awfully chipper."

It's impossible to hide anything from her. I looked anywhere but at her, "Ummm... brunch." I mumbled.

She shook her head sadly as she left. "Be careful, Krustallos. See ya in a few hours, sis."

I waved even though she was already out of my room, "Bye Bevi. Love you." I heard a, "You better!" as the condo door closed.

Clothes! I must have had half my closet on the floor of my bedroom before I went to my dresser and pulled out some bleached white jeans, torn in strategic locations to show off my legs. Then a spaghetti strap pink half shirt. I topped it with a plain white long sleeved blouse I rescued from my floor and tied it at my tummy, showing off my abs and bellybutton enticingly and the sleeves rolled to my elbow.

I checked myself out in the bathroom floor full length mirror, then slipped on some white ankle socks and my pink converse. I did a quick touch up of my makeup and verified my messy ponytail was arranged correctly... I pulled an extra few strands on my right side to hang down the length of my neck. *There, looks casual but still temping.*

My phone buzzed. I took it off the charger and read the text from Riley. *[outside]* I smiled and responded. *[on way out]* I grabbed my purse and ran out the door and down the stairs. When I turned into the lobby I slowed to a casual walk.

I stepped outside and there she was idling at the curb. I couldn't stop my huge smile. I gave her a tiny wave and got in the car, just to be rewarded with her butterfly inducing smile. Her casual look was stunning, and I'm sure, just as planned as my look. She wore tight jeans with a wide pink belt, a bright yellow belly shirt that looked painted on, and a matching wide pink hairband. She was stunning.

"Hey." I said.

She grinned. "Hey back." I just smiled as she pulled away from the curb.

She kept glancing at me until she finally said, "So are you going to keep me in suspense forever or are you going to tell me where we're eating brunch?"

I laughed out loud at that. Then I had it, "Oh, I have an idea, lets hit Pike Place." She grinned and jumped back on the freeway and we shot toward the city.

I saw her iPod in the receiver and started going through the play list, she was eyeballing me as I did. I smiled again at what I saw. "I thought I loved music, you seem to have a little of everything!"

She looked pleased as she said, "Music is one of my passions."

She was about to continue when I squealed, "Oh my God! I didn't think anyone else had ever heard of Vixen and 'Edge of a Broken Heart'!" I hit play and cranked the car stereo.

To my extreme pleasure she started singing at the top of her lungs with me. We spent the ride to Pike Place Market that way. Me hunting up obscure music and us shouting them out, laughing and having a great time. We actually got lucky and caught a parking spot on the street, thank goodness for Sunday, as we finished belting out Gloria Gaynor's 'I Will Survive'.

We sat giggling for a minute, it was a comfortable silence. Finally I broke it while staring at my cellphone, "That... was fun." She nodded agreement enthusiastically as I kept staring at my phone.

Then she asked, "Expecting a call or something?"

I held my finger up. "Or something." I counted down with my fingers 3, 2, 1 and the official market bell went off signaling 9:00 opening time. "That." I laughed and hopped out of the car.

She stepped out of the car and just stood there with her door opened looking over the car at me, shaking her head and smiling. "You really are something." She shut her door and walked around to me as I blushed.

We simultaneously reached for each others hand laced our fingers, then I was off, dragging her quickly toward the 'Post Alley' buildings. She was laughing. "Where are we going, Cryster?"

I just shot her a coy smile as we slid past the triangle building and into a side door on the building across the courtyard, then down the hall to a new restaurant/bakery 'The Pike'. I did a big jump the last two steps and did a 'taa-daa' movement with my hands toward the door.

"Welcome to The Pike my question-y friend!" I opened the glass door for her to step in, the aroma of fresh baked bread sneaking out. A grandmotherly woman who was finishing setting up the four little two seat expanded metal patio tables, looked over and smiled and started walking up to Riley. Then she saw me and her smile brightened even more, moving over to pull me into a quick hug. "Crystal! Hello dear, how have you been?"

"Same ol, same ol, Mrs. Zatta. I'd like you to meet Jane. She's a very *SPECIAL* friend of mine." I said with a motion toward Riley. She stretched out and snagged Riley and pulled her into a quick hug then I grabbed Riley's hand again.

"Very nice to meet you Jane!" Mrs. Z said, then she looked at our hands and said in a fake hushed tone and a wink to me, obviously wanting Riley to hear, "She's quite the looker. I didn't know you swung that way, Crystal." Riley blushed.

I just waggled my eyebrows, "You never know." I said cryptically. I could see Riley trying to read into it unsuccessfully, cocking a perfectly sculpted brow. Then I said, "We decided to do a breakfast slash brunch thing here today. Whatcha got for us? Oh by the way, I found a guy that can service your broken Swedish dough mixer. He owes me a favor so he'll be here tomorrow, free of charge, just need to pay for any parts."

Mrs. Z brightened, "Bless your heart, I don't know how you find these people. Well do you girls want menus or want me to surprise you." She looked over at Riley at the last part. Riley's expressions were giving her face a case of whiplash. First interest in the mixer dilemma, then surprise at my solution, then hungry excitement at the prospect of food.

"Please Mrs. Zatta, by all means, surprise us. It smells heavenly in here," she replied excitedly.

This was the right answer and Mrs. Z brightened and scurried off as we sat at a table, calling over her shoulder, "Please Jane, call me Emily. Two breakfast bowl's coming up!"

I took the time to look this beautiful brunette over again as she was watching Mrs. Z go. She made casual look so... sexy? Easy? Well whatever it was, it worked for her. Then her swirling chocolate brow eyes swung toward me and captured my gaze. Suddenly I got shy at being caught checking her out. "Ummm.. hi?"

She laughed gently, "Hi... So how do you know Emily?" she asked tilting her head in genuine curiosity.

I smiled at the look. "She supplied some fresh baked bread from a portable wood fired brick oven at one of my parties. The people that didn't have a food-gasm from the fresh baked bread smell, stood in line forever just for a small taste of it."

"She is such a sweet lady. She had told me she was looking for a permanent location but rent in the core is spendy. I knew a guy here at the market that owed me a favor, I secured this location for her at half market rate." I finished.

She laughed sweetly, it was like a melody. "Of course you knew a guy. You are pretty amazing there, Cryster." I blushed.

To save me from dying of embarrassment or professing my undying love to Riley, it was a tossup on which, Mrs. Z showed up with a tray. It contained two fresh baked bread bowls filled with scrambled eggs, diced ham, peppers, and onions all smothered in a white gravy. A carafe of fresh squeezed orange juice with glasses and a pot of fresh brewed coffee with two mugs.

"Bon appetit ladies." she said excitedly as she smiled, standing expectantly by the table. I took the cue and took a large fork full, Riley did the same. The satisfied groans from us were what she was waiting for and she scurried off satisfied.

Riley moaned again on a second bite, "Oh my God. This is better than sex."

I giggled, "Then you aren't doing it right."

Riley almost spit out her food, and I continued, "But this is fan-friggin-tabulous." I reached over and poured us juice and coffee and took a large swig of orange juice. This was wonderful.

We had a relaxed meal, another couple came in and sat at the far side of the bakery as we continued our easy conversations. She was such an interesting conversationalist and kept me engaged and laughing the whole meal. I noticed a street performer setting up through the window and made a mental note.

When we were stuffed and our bread bowls, soaked in the luscious gravy, were torn apart and devoured, Mrs. Z had materialized again and started clearing our table. She smiled and said, "Now you girls go and enjoy this marvelous day, and thanks for coming in."

Riley was reaching for her purse and wallet as Mrs. Z was tottering off. I placed my hand gently on her hand, stopping her and whispering, "Our money is no good here. You'd be insulting her if you paid. She's a proud woman and we just trade in favors." She nodded understanding and gave me a look that melted me inside.

As we made our way to the door, Mrs. Z came puttering over for hugs from the both of us. Then I said, "Hey, Mrs. Zatta, could you get Mike out there a loaf for his family? I owe him one and hate being on that end of the trading scale."

She looked out the window at the street performer juggling everything *INCLUDING* a kitchen sink and smiled. "More than happy to, when he found out last week I knew you, he has been setting up out in front every day to attract customers for me. We all gotta look out for each other. Now off with you two. It was an extreme pleasure meeting you Jane. Crystal *NEVER* brings anyone around besides her wonderful sister, Beverly."

I saw the look on Riley's face at that revelation. But she recovered quickly. "The pleasure was all mine, Emily."

As we walked back outside, Riley tuned to me with a thoughtful look as I waved to Mike. She spoke carefully, "You all really do look out for each other don't you?"

I smiled, "It's the only way to network. Find good people that can help good people and everyone is happy."

She took the opportunity to return my hand to its rightful place... in hers. I leaned up and gave her a quick peck on the lips then asked, "You mind if we do a quick detour to the Main Arcade over there for a little example of my networking?" I quirked an eyebrow at her.

Her smile couldn't have been more genuine as I saw it twinkling in her eyes. "Lead on, Macbeth."

We got to the fish mongers and I grabbed a couple disposable gloves sitting in a stack by an ice bed and slid them on and looked up just as a fish was sailing through the air to me. Riley gasped, but I deftly caught it. Seven pounds at least. I winked at the monger that tossed it and examined the salmon, checking its gills and just tossed it right back.

"Looks good, Sam, can you get two over to Alessandro's today? I owe him for a marker I pulled in," I said as I was taking the gloves back off and tossing them in the trashcan beside me. Riley looked impressed. That made me bite my lower lip.

Sam shot back, "You got it Miss James! So I lost track, does this make us even?"

I giggled as I reached into my purse and pulled out two concert tickets. "Only if you and Mary don't want front row tickets to Kirby Monroe on Friday."

He wiped his hands on his apron as he walked quickly around the counter and snatched the tickets from me. "No way! These have been sold out for a month, where did you get these?" He asked as he stuffed them in his pocket.

Riley seemed to be having a great time as she was starting to giggle herself as she answered before I could, "She knows a guy." Shooting him a wink and causing me to snort.

Sam looked at her then to me. "Oh this isn't Bev... who is this lovely lady, Miss James?"

I slapped his muscular shoulder playfully. "Hey, eyes front sailor! You got Mary. Miss McKay here is mine!" Sam grinned and raised his hands in defeat as Riley looked happily shocked at my statement.

Riley blushed, it looked way too cute and was causing a blush of my own. I grabbed Riley's soft, warm hand and started back toward the car. "See ya Sam. Remember to say hi to Mary for me." He waved as we walked away.

We got back to the car and stood for a minute, but I didn't want my time with Riley to end so I said, "Ok you suffered through my markers. Now I belong to you. What do you wanna do?"

She smiled and put her keys back in her purse, then linked arms with me and started leading me down the block. "Well I have some ideas. I'm really enjoying these glimpses into your world. It sounds as if you never bring anyone around except Beverly, and they all think she is your sister."

I shrugged, "Yeah, she's always called me 'sis' after our kissing incident, and she pretty much is my sister, so it's easier to let them think that than having to correct them all the time. *AND*, there has never been anyone else in my life I wanted them to meet." I blushed at my admission.

She stopped walking and turned to look into my eyes, it was like gravity pulling me in, she leaned down and captured my lips gently with hers. Swooning is so easy with her. Then she broke the kiss leaving me like a fish gasping for air. She smiled that she got the desired effect. "Come on!" she laughed and dragged me along, me riding on my personal cloud nine.

A couple blocks later she stopped a a little red door between two shops in a two story brick building. She opened the door, revealing a narrow, steep stairway leading up. She smiled and shooed me in. "I noticed you had some vinyl at your place last night. I'm amazed you seem to love music as much as I do, that's rare, normally I drive my girlfriends crazy with it."

I almost passed out happy at the word girlfriend. If only she really felt that way. This relationship is so confusing to me, but then again, she does keep reminding me it is just a game to her. We reached the top of the stairs and she lead me to the right. And there it was, Record Nirvana, a shop with rows upon rows upon rows of vinyl records. All vintage and tons of imports.

I stood unmoving. Was this a mirage? I've seen plenty of vintage record shops but this place was huge! She laughed at me musically and whispered in my ear, her hot breath causing goosebumps to dance their way happily down my flesh. "Come on in, let's see what booty we can find."

She dragged me in like she was pulling a small child. That's how I felt. I saw an isle labeled 45's. I drooled and made my way over. "Oooo, nice choice!" she said laughingly beside me.

I looked at her and bit my lower lip as I started playing with the end of my ponytail and turned excitedly to the racks started happily flipping through some vintage imports.

"So what types of bands are you..." I interrupted her with a squeal as I held up a single triumphantly. I held it out to her with both hands, she looked and quirked an eyebrow as I giggled. "I've been looking for this single forever! Finding anything from the Divinyls 80's years is hard enough, with them being Australian and all, but 'Back to the Wall'! Most people only know their song 'I Touch Myself'."

She had a permanent smile on her face watching my antics as she pulled out an Apple label Beatles single 'Oh Darling' and held it out to me triumphantly and said, "Ha! This completes my Apple label Beatles 45's this one doesn't even have a catalog number, and is oh so rare! 'Here Comes the Sun' is the flip side."

We both bounced around like a couple teenagers at our

discovered treasure. I continued flipping through records until I stopped on one and pulled it to my chest. She looked at me with curiosity as I said, "Please don't hate me... and don't judge me." I held the single out with both hands for her to see, my head hung low.

She started laughing and hugged me in apology as she stuttered out between laughs, "The Bangles? Eternal Flame?" She wiped a happy tear from her eye.

Then she straightened up at the sight of my pouty lower lip. "Sorry, not judging." She suppressed a laugh. Then she quirked one of those marvelous eyebrows I am so obsessed with and added, "You know, I've noticed that all your favorite songs or bands are either girl bands or have female leads. Whether it is at the club, on the radio, on my iPod or here digging through the vinyl. You seem to like and awful lot of women. You *SURE* you're not gay?"

For you. I started playing with my ponytail. "I'm not sure of much anymore," then bit my lower lip.

"Damn." she whispered, "You really have to stop doing that. I can't be held responsible if I kiss you when you do."

I flushed, I was hot everywhere. "Then kiss me," I said simply as I leaned in and we shared our gentlest, sweetest kiss yet.

I smiled coyly and went back to digging up buried treasure. It took her a few seconds before she followed suit, I could hear that her ragged breathing matched mine. Over the next hour we found a couple more 45's each.

We talked and joked and shared our musical tastes, which were very similar except she had male bands mixed in with the real good stuff. I was starting to replay her observation and her question. Maybe I knew I was gay all along but never shared it with my conscious mind.

We went up to pay and a guy who looked to be someone from a punk band throwback to the 1980's brightened up. "Hey, Jane. What ya got to spin today? I located that Lynyrd Skynyrd triple 3 album you put that bodacious bounty on. Should be here this week."

She smiled. "Sweet!" She handed over her booty to him and grabbed my 45's before I could protest. Then she continued as he rung us up, "Just filling some holes in the collection."

He replied, "Cool. That's like twenty four thirty three, Jane." She looked at him like he was speaking Swahili. He faltered then started punching things on the register, "Fifteen twenty two?"

She cleared her throat, "Golly Seth, where did you get that still sealed, mint White Album there in that glass case behind the counter?"

He slumped his shoulders and punched some stuff on the register. "With my employee discount that's eight fifty two."

She grinned like a Cheshire cat and handed him a ten spot. "Keep the change." He smiled back at both of us.

It was obvious that this was a game they played frequently at checkout. I felt an odd sort of pride for her having the upper hand in the negotiation. It's always good to be on the owed side and not the owing when it comes to favors. Markers are better than cash. They are my currency. She's a girl after my own heart. *She can have mine if she wants it.*

As we were marching down the stairs we glanced at each other and started cracking up. Then she spoke my own thoughts, "I can see why you like to keep the upper hand in your networking, it comes in useful."

I just grinned at her. I started back toward the car and she grabbed my hand dragging me the opposite location, toward the Space Needle. "One last stop," She laughed.

I'd let her lead me anywhere as long as she doesn't let my hand go. Then I started cracking up again as she started humming Eternal Flame.

By the time we reached the Space Needle we were half way walking, half way dramatically gesturing and belting out the full chorus of Eternal Flame and everyone around us were either smiling or avoiding us like we were insane.

She pointed across the street grinning, I followed her finger and her gaze to the amphibious duck boats. My grin got bigger than hers, and the absurdity that we were acting like tourists in our own city turned that grin into a full blown smile.

We walked across the street hand in hand and she pulled us to one side to where a very cute girl in a duck tour uniform was standing. Then Riley bumped her knees to the back of the girl's knees, almost making the girl fall down.

When the radiant blonde turned around she squealed and almost jumped on Riley and hugged her, Riley never letting go of me. "Jane! Oh my God! How are you?" the blonde girl bubbled.

Riley smiled back. "Doing great, Sandra! So, can you hook a

girl up? Trying to impress here."

The blonde looked like she was about to explode into cuteness when she looked at me then our hands. She leaned in like they were doing a covert operation and slid two passes into Riley's hand and whispering waaaaay too loudly, "OMG she's cute! And those eyes!"

I was blushing again as Riley pulled me into the line to board a Duck, calling over her shoulder, "Thanks, San! You're the best!"

I looked back and saw the girl was smiling and blushing redder than I was and looking at her shoes. I felt a tinge of jealousy and looked a question up into Riley's eyes.

She smiled reassuringly. "No, not an ex. Old friend of the family. She's sorta crushed on me since we were like five, but we never dated. She is one of the sweetest girls you will ever meet, but sadly, was sort of passed over in the smarts department. I like my girls to challenge me intellectually. I sorta look out for her whenever I see her at the clubs, too many people willing to take advantage of a sweet, naive girl like her."

My opinion of Riley just went up another notch. *Is that even possible?* I pulled her down for a quick peck on the lips before we boarded the vehicle. Now I'm not too proud to admit that I clung to her like a little kid when we drove down into the water. I was a little nervous. I mean, cars aren't supposed to ride the waves you know.

I nervously twisted the end of my ponytail until we were well underway. Then I just sort of naturally melted into Riley's arms as the tour progressed. She traced lazy circles on the exposed flesh of my belly with her thumbs as we looked at the city from the water. This was so easy with her, so natural. We didn't talk we just enjoyed the tour and the closeness of each other.

I was sad when the tour was over, I had to leave her arms. But we had a blast trying to stump each other with music trivia walking back to the car. I stopped before getting in, "You were pretty terrific today, you got a nice web of contacts yourself. Showoff." I winked at her.

She just gave me an eye sparkling smile that made my legs turn to jelly. "Well I can't have you showing me up all the time now can I?" I started playing with my ponytail and got in the car.

Before she started the car she turned to me with a cockeyed tilt to her head and a reflective smile. I grinned at her, "What?"

She crinkled her nose and said, "You really don't know you're doing it do you?" I looked at her tilting my head, prompting for more information. She shook her head with a little laugh. "That adorable thing you do with your hair." I looked at my ponytail between my fingers and dropped it self consciously. Which just made me want to start playing with my ponytail. *Damn vicious circle!*

She laughed a melodious laugh as she read all this in my face. I looked at my hands and started playing with my fingers. "Sorry it's just a nervous habit."

Riley smiled, shaking her head in contemplation. "Actually I'd say three distinct habits." Wow, Bevi told me that once too, but I didn't know anyone else could read me like her.

She continued, "You roll the hair between your fingers and your eyes widen slightly when you are nervous. Then you kind of slide the strands across each other and you drop your eyelids slightly when you get shy or bashful. Both of which makes me want to... I don't know... hug you and protect you?" She smiled like she had just unraveled one of the secrets of the universe.

I cocked an eyebrow. "You said three. That was two." She bit her lower lip. *Doesn't she know what that does to me?*

"Well that one is the one I both hate and love," she replied,

"When you get coy and seductive you twirl the end absentmindedly and bite your lower lip and do something with your eyes that I can't explain. The effect is devastating and I have to fight myself to keep from throwing you down on the ground and having my way with you right there." She looked embarrassed at the admission.

I was blushing profusely and overly aroused at that. "You should." I slapped my hands to my mouth. *Holy crap! Why do I keep saying things out loud!?* She had a shocked look on her face. I wanted to crawl into a hole.

"That's cute too," she confessed. I reached for my ponytail and realized I was doing it and dropped my hand.

Her expression was unreadable as she started the car. She saw my hesitation and said quietly, "Don't be self conscious about it," then quieter still, "I like it." I gave her a nervous smile. Then she brightened up and put on some girl band music for me. The ride home was awesome, we once again had our own private karaoke session, laughing and singing. Though there was a shadow of confusion lurking in my mind.

We got to my place and she idled by the curb, our hands found each others, our fingers finding themselves laced as they should be. I brought hers to my lips and kissed each finger. "I'm sorry things got weird there, sometimes my damn mouth has a mind of its own."

She leaned in close and placed her forehead on mine. "It's OK. It's just a game after all. And this doesn't count as a date!" Her eyes were twinkling with humor. I'm sure mine went dull from her reminder that this isn't real to her.

I tried to stay cheerful. "Uhh, yeah. Too bad, third date entitled you to some over the sweater action." I winked.

A mixture of lust and disappointment twinkled in her eyes. "Damn!" she muttered almost under her breath.

This caused me to bite my lower lip and to start playing with my ponytail. I realized I was doing it when her eyes went wide, she opened her mouth to say something. I dropped it quickly and we laughed until I shut her up by kissing her softly.

I broke the kiss and pulled my forehead from hers. Missing the contact already. Then I shot her a cocky smile. "I'll be damned. It works, it does shut people up." She slapped my arm with a grin. I looked at her, not wanting the day to end. "Umm... so I guess I'll call you later to set up the next date?" She looked as sad about leaving too and nodded.

I got out of the car and offered a smile and a tiny wave. She smiled and did the same as she drove off. I had just unlocked the door to enter the lobby when my phone buzzed. It was a text from Riley, I could still see her car receding down the street. *[bored]* To my shame, I snorted. Then I shot back *[chick flick?]* and got an almost immediate answer *[b right up :)]*.

Chapter 7 – Blurring of the Line

We were snuggled in on the couch under a blanket, munching on popcorn, my head resting in the crook of her neck watching 'Imagine Me and You' when the door opened. Bev came in already talking, holding a big box, "Kru if you didn't get you some of that fine... oh, hi. Jane!" Bev did a bad job of acting innocent.

We were both grinning at her from the couch. Her eyes shot to the TV, her favorite movie, to the popcorn, her favorite snack, to the blanket, her favorite... "Snuggle time!" she yelled as she put her box down and hopped over the back of the couch to lay her head in our laps as she helped herself to a handful of popcorn. It was impossible for Riley and I not to laugh.

Bevi asked with a mouthful of popcorn, "Dey at dah danfce scuheen yet?"

Riley surprised me with her Beverly decoding capability, "Nope, dance scene coming up." Then she turned to me with an amused grin, "She really *IS* like this isn't she?" I giggled and nodded and we all relaxed to watch the rest of the show.

Riley's hand was lightly brushing along my side under the blanket as we watched. It was doing amazing things to me. I let an arm drift back and started lazily tracing circles on Riley's hip with my fingernails, keeping an eye on Bev to make sure she didn't notice.

I think Riley took this as a challenge, I glanced back to see her grin as she kept one eye on Bevi as well. Then she moved her hand a little higher and I stopped breathing as the side of her hand grazed the side of my breast. When I remembered to breath again I slowly wiggled my hand into her tight jean pocket, and curled my fingers slowly toward her hip, causing my nails to drag along her flesh with much more pressure, only the pocket lining protecting her, I heard her breath hitch. Ha! Point for me!

She, placed her chin on top of my head and blatantly punished me for that by cupping my breast. This time my breath hitched. All brain function stopped, and I lived only in the feel of her thumb tracing little circles on the side of my breast through the fabric of my shirt and bra.

That's how we spent the rest of the movie. I was unmoving and silent, frozen, feeling her attention on the side of my breast, not wanting to do anything that might cause her to stop and Bev and Riley spent the rest of the movie making commentary and joking. Riley was even relaxed enough around Beverly now to play lazily with her hair with her other hand. I'm not sure I even took a breath the whole movie, my hand still curled in her pocket.

Happy warmth buzzing through me.

I wanted to look back at her, but thought she might stop if I did. I could feel the heat of her hand cupping me through the shirt and bra, like they weren't even there. I'm sure I was sweating. Then I heard something. The thumb stopped moving and Riley's total domination over me loosened enough for me to realize Bev was talking to me.

"Earth to Krustallos! I was asking, if you were gay, would you go after Luce or Rachel in the show?" she asked.

Why is it so hot in here? I stuttered out, "Umm I don't know. Rachel seems so high maintenance. So, probably Luce, I mean she's hot and would probably own me in bed." *Like Riley just owned me on the couch.* I tried to play along, "So what did you two choose?"

Bev laughed, "Where the hell have you been? It's been the topic of conversation for the last ten minutes."

I blushed and shot an evil look back at Riley. "Ummm... I was just a little distracted." I heard a little snort from Riley. I went to sit up and pull my hand out of her pocket, but she started with her thumb again and I forgot what I was doing as I melted in to her again.

I looked back into her eyes, and they were sparkling with mischief. *Crap, she knows she has control here.* Riley spoke up, "So, ladies. Another movie? Or spin some vinyl?"

God, I couldn't survive another two hours of this torture. So I forced my mouth to work through the happy fog created by Riley's assault on my flesh, "Let's listen to some albums or the singles we got today."

At that, Riley gently squeezed her hand a bit, causing me to gasp, then released me and pulled her hand out from under the blanket saying, "Oooo sounds like fun!" This was my punishment from her for suggesting it, and I knew it, removal of my silent, beautiful torture.

Bev rolled off the couch and onto all fours on the floor before standing and wandering toward her room mumbling "God, no. Now there's two of them." Then she called over her shoulder as she grabbed her box and brought it into her room, "If you two think you can torture me with ancient mono track music from bands that are like in their 50's and 60's or older now, you're wrong. I'll be in here if you need me." And she shut her door to our giggles.

Riley smiled and whispered, "Looks like I got my over the

sweater action after all. You shouldn't have escalated the cold war." She bit her lower lip and winked. I'm sure I melted again as I blushed and stood to make my way over to my vinyl record collection.

I hoarsely whispered back, "My God woman, it was all I could do to not squirm and moan! I was scared to death with Bevi there!"

She chuckled, proud of both herself and my reaction as she stood and made her way over to me and the records. I grabbed a 33-1/3 album, not showing her, and put it on my phonograph and fired up my old tube amplifier.

She quirked a perfectly sculpted eyebrow at that, saying, "Wow! I didn't know those things still existed!"

I smiled at her coyly. "Gives a much richer seductive tone to the vinyl, solid state amps are too harsh. I mean you like seductive over harsh don't you?" I quirked an eyebrow and she just bit her lower lip in retaliation to my implication. *She fights dirty!*

I put the needle gently on the vinyl and cranked the volume 'Til You're Dead' by Melissa Ferrick blasted out the speakers. This got a huge smile out of Riley. I quickly realized she had never heard it as I started dancing with her, belting it out. I gathered that her smile was because, yet again, it was a female singer. *I can't help it, I like what I like.*

Once the song was over, we stopped dancing and I stopped the record before the next song and pulled it off. She was thumbing through my treasure trove as I slid the album back in its sleeve. She swung her eyes up to me in mirth and said, "Seriously Cryster, there isn't a single album in here that doesn't have a female lead. I think I've found your kryptonite!"

"You certainly did earlier," I mumbled under my breath.

She grinned smugly, "I certainly did." *Damn her and her freakishly good hearing!* I blushed again and started playing with my ponytail.

We spent the next hour just spinning vinyl and dancing, laughing, and having fun. I noticed our dancing was getting closer and more seductive as each song went along. We were taking turns selecting songs, and each one got slower and slower. Until I was in her arms, with my head resting on her chest. Our arms around each other and just swaying with the music, not really even dancing.

I started crying, and I don't have any clue why. When Riley noticed she brought me over to the couch, her face etched with concern and dried my tears asking, "What is it Cryster? What's wrong?"

I just shrugged and smiled through bleary eyes. "I really don't know. But today has been... nice. Maybe I'm just getting confused or something. What part of *US* is just that dumbass bet and how much of this is real?"

This changed her posture, she pulled away slightly and put her hands in her lap. Was it something I said? I hope she doesn't realize I had fallen for her, I know she doesn't feel the same. Then she confirmed it "Right... just a game." Then she stood. "I'd better get going. Thanks for such a fun day. I guess I'll hear from you soon about the next date?" She started moving toward the door quickly.

I nodded at her as I stood to follow. Damn, I had ruined such a great day. One of the best days of my life if I am to be honest with myself.

I brightened up, "Oh, wait. Parking in the lot is spendy. Here... use this whenever you come over!" I grabbed my purse and dug around and pulled out a few one month parking passes and handed her one, she took it between two fingers, squinting her eyes. Then she eyeballed the rest as I put them back away.

She cocked her perfectly sculpted eyebrow. "Let me guess, you know a guy?"

We both laughed as I nodded. I was happy I could still get her to smile.

I wasn't even thinking when she opened the door and turned back to say goodbye, when I leaned up and gave her a passionate goodnight kiss. When I realized it I broke the kiss, embarrassed. "G-goodnight Riley. I really had fun today, thanks."

She gave me a smile tinged with sadness in her eyes, "Me too. Good night, Crystal."

I shut the door behind her and leaned my back against it, realizing she didn't use her nickname for me. It was still early, but I wandered into Bev's dungeon and she looked up from where she was reading on her iPad at her desk to see my eyes brimming with tears and wordlessly hopped into her bed and held the covers open for me to slide in with her.

She hugged me protectively and whispered, "You gotta put a stop to this, Kru."

I shrugged and whispered back, "I know. But I can't, at least this way I still get to see her. Just one more date. If I can't handle it anymore I'll just quit."

Then I spoke into the air, more at the universe than to Bev, "Sometimes I feel like she feels it too. I mean it seems so real. But then she clams up and reminds me it isn't. My blurry line is just black and white to her." She shook her head and just held me, rocking me.

We sat like that for a long time just comforting each other over our doomed relationships. Silently communicating a whole conversation, complete with arguments, realizations and resignation to the inevitable outcomes of her relationship with Lori and mine with Riley, just from our familiarity with each other. I finally dozed off, thanking the powers that be for my best friend, my sister from another mother that is Beverly.

Chapter 8 – Third Date

Monday morning rolled around and I glanced at Bev's alarm clock, 8:15am, we had slept over twelve hours. I poked Bev who just groaned, "Whhhhaaaaaaat?" I poked her again, stating, "Rise and shine, Bevi. You're going to be late for work."

She looked at the clock and groaned again, "I didn't set the damn alarm last night."

She rolled off the bed and stood and started unabashedly stripping naked as she made her way toward her attached bathroom. I called after her as I stood, "Breakfast?" I got a zombie groan in return, that's code for "Yes please, and thank you." in Bevi land. I smiled and wandered into the kitchen and got out two bowls, and poured some of my Fruit Loops, from my hidden stash, into them and put spoons by the bowls. *Yes, the hidden stash that Bev knows about!* Then I started the coffee.

A few minutes later zombie Bev dragged herself out to the kitchen wearing her uniform. I grabbed the milk from the fridge and she brightened up, seeing my Fruit Loops in her bowl as I poured the milk in.

"Oooo my favorite!" she chirped.

This caused me to chuckle. "No, you mean *MY* favorite."

She grinned like a chipmunk, her cheeks filled with sugary goodness, and mumbled out, "Tomato tomatoh." Then she punctuated it by scooping up another big bite.

I poured her a large coffee in a disposable cup and snapped the sip lid on it. I giggled, I felt like I was getting my child ready for school. She read me like a book as always and grabbed the cup as she headed toward the door, kissing my cheek, "Thanks, mom!" We both chuckled and I called after her, "Don't accept any rides from strangers! And come straight home after school, young lady!" We shared another laugh as she shut the door behind her.

I cleaned up the breakfast dishes and headed toward my room to get ready for the day.

- - -

I was clean, refreshed and dressed by 9:30 and grabbed my cell. *[got plans 2day?]* I shot to Riley. Moments later she shot back *[just waiting on yr date invite :)]* I laughed, she was so sure of herself and her charms. *Well she has reason to be.* I shot back my customary *[call me]* and my phone started ringing.

I answered, "Consider yourself invited, I'll be there in 30."

She laughed then she said, "You know, this is like four days in a row, people are going to talk."

I laughed back, "Let them talk. You gonna be ready? Just casual, but you will need a jacket."

I could hear the smile in her voice. "Oooo another day date. I'm ready already. See ya soon, Cryster," and she hung up.

I found myself smiling. She used the nickname again! Maybe she isn't mad about how I ruined the night after all. I got to my car and got a [bored] text on my cell. I smiled and fired back [call me] Then I answered the ringing on speakerphone, "Hey, girl! Why you so bored?" She giggled like a madwoman at the expected greeting.

She sounded nonchalant, "Oh, no reason. Just waiting for some chick to bring me on a mystery date."

I smiled, "Anyone I know?"

She played along. "Just some girl with a ponytail. Didn't get her name."

We continued the banter until I was descending the exit ramp with me saying, "Getting off the exit now, see you in five." I was rewarded with a super cute, "K, bye," and she hung up. I approached her loft and saw her standing on the sidewalk with her thumb out. I smiled to myself then I pulled up and she hopped in with a grin.

She grabbed my hand and our fingers found their rightful configuration. Then she chirped, "Hi!"

I was grinning like a fool as I replied, "I'm not supposed to pickup hitchhikers."

She mocked indignation. "Fine, return me to my stoop, driver," while placing the back of her hand on her forehead dramatically.

This got a chuckle from me. "For all you know I'm some psycho hitchhiker picker-upper who will drive you somewhere to take away your innocence."

She sat up straight and her smile returned. "You say that as if it is a bad thing!"

We shared a laugh as we continued deeper into downtown, I turned on Pike and she laughed, "Again?"

That was the desired response, so I waggled my eyebrows as we drove right past the market. This got me a, "Tease!" from the brunette vixen. Then I veered east and asked, "I assume you had breakfast already?" She responded with, "One of those granola bars that seem to be all over my loft and office, I swear I don't know where they keep coming from. Oh, and some coffee."

I smiled. "Good, then you'll be hungry at lunch." She still had curiosity painted all across her face as we got on the northbound Interstate 5. I fessed up a little, "Well, this may lose your whole bet thing for me here. This is more of a day trip that my parents would take me on when I was little, I have some fond memories and just wanted to share a little of my childhood with you. So no spectacularly romantic gestures. Just me." I finished sheepishly.

She looked almost moved as she spoke quietly, "Sharing personal memories is one of the most powerful romantic gestures there is. So... we've never talked about your parents. They live here?"

I shook my head. "No my mother got offered a CIO position down in San Jose five years ago and off they went. I stayed since I had a scholarship to UW. I even had Vee Jacobs, the poet, in my freshman English Lit class. *SHE* was an inspiring girl. I love this city, so here I stay."

She looked thoughtful, and I asked, "How about your folks?"

She shrugged, "Just mom and I back in DC. Dad took off when I came out at fifteen. Mom already knew when I told her. She never wavered. I love that woman. When I came to Seattle on a vacation a few years back, I fell in love with the city and the Cascade Mountains, so I sort of never went back. I don't get to see my mom as much as I'd like, but she's happy."

I was absorbing everything she said, I realized I had been silent for too long after she finished. "I'm sorry about your father. I don't know why it makes a damn bit of difference if someone is straight or gay, they are the exact same person they were before they came out. I just hope that if I ever determine whether or not I'm a lesbian, that I don't lose someone I love that way."

I saw her squint at the 'whether or not', trying to read into it. I don't know why I'm so scared to just admit to her that I've come to the determined that I am. I have never connected with another person like I do with her. It goes beyond the connection I have with Bev. I'm just scared that she doesn't feel it too. *Coward.*

She finally spoke, "How would your parent's take it if you did?" She tilted her head and squeezed my hand. I guess she could tell I was in heavy thought over the subject. I glanced over and our eyes met for a moment, I got an electric charge from her swirling chocolate browns intensely searching my duo-tone eyes for clues.

I took a breath as I looked back at the road. "They'd actually be pretty fine with it. After Bevi came out, my parent's didn't treat her any different. They love her like a daughter and I swear that my mom thought I was gay too and was trying to get us together for months after that. Then she would even point out pretty girls for me all the time, 'Oooo look at that one honey. She's hot isn't she?'. I think she kind of figured it out though, seeing the string of boys I'd bring home."

She snickered. "I think I already like your mom."

I smiled and offhandedly replied, "You should come on down the next time I go to visit them." I kicked myself for saying my thoughts out loud again, what the heck is wrong with me?

She stopped for a second or two, reading me, then said softly, "I'd like that." Catching me off guard.

I smiled at her as I slid onto the Highway 525 interchange to Mukilteo. "Almost there." She glanced at the signs then looked a question at me. I chuckled. "Patience my inquisitive Riley. All shall be revealed soon." I winked an she shook her head at me smiling.

I turned on the radio and cued up some girl bands on my iPod, much to her amusement. "Hey, don't judge me," I giggled. And a few minutes later we were pulling up to the Mukilteo Lighthouse Park. I smiled hugely at her as I parked the car.

"We're heeeeeere," I called out as we hopped out of the car. She looked one part amused and one part curious as I grabbed her hand and dragged her toward the lighthouse, saying, "My dad has this thing for lighthouses. He'd tell me the story of every one we'd visit. Mukilteo is special, since it is still in operation."

"In a time of electronic warning systems, radar and sonar, lighthouses serve no purpose, but the sailors around here still swear that they navigate by it at night and it gives them a certain feeling of protection seeing its gleaming warning," I repeated what my father told me when I was eight.

"He brought me here for the first time when I was in the fourth grade. I don't know how he pulled it off, but instead of the regular tour, he got us up to the lens room to look out over the Sound. I think he knew the caretaker or something."

I could see amusement in her eyes, I read into it and made a connection I had never seen before this moment. Then I laughed out loud, "Seems I may have just discovered where my networking inspiration came from. I guess he 'knew a guy'." She seriously laughed out loud at that.

"Now, let's do the tour!" I was excited as we went through the ground level, listening to the history of the lighthouse from the thirty year old lady with the Mukilteo Historical Society uniform on. She spoke of the difference between the fixed Fresnel lens it has now and the old revolving Fresnel lens it replaced. How sailors can still see the light beam from twelve nautical miles away. We were in tourist mode and shared smiling glances back and forth, bumping hips and having fun, just soaking in the ambiance.

An older couple gave us quite a dirty look when they saw we were holing hands and being so familiar with each other. Riley tried to let go of my hand, I could read it in her eyes that she didn't want people looking at me that way. I wouldn't let her let go and gave her a reassuring squeeze and I raised our hands and kissed the back of her's, which got me a warm smile in trade. Then we chuckled at the old folks as they jockeyed to move up to the front of the tour, away from us.

When the tour was over and everyone was filing out, I pulled Riley off to the side. When everyone was gone the tour operator turned around and beamed a giant smile at me, "Crystal! Long time no see!" She looked at Riley then stopped for a second,

"Oh, this isn't your sister, Bev."

I smiled back and released Riley's hand to give the girl a hug, "Hi Leanna. I'd like you to meet Jane McKay. I thought I'd bring her on a date here, exploring my childhood a bit."

Leanna didn't even bat an eyelash at the word 'date' as she turned to Riley and surprised her with a hug, "Very pleased to meet you, Jane. You must be a special girl. Crystal *NEVER* brings anyone around."

She released the hug and Riley smiled at her and replied, "I've been hearing that a lot lately," then she reclaimed my hand... and my heart... for her own again. I blushed at Riley and bit my lower lip, and started playing with my ponytail with my other hand. Then I turned to Leanna. "So, would it be possible to... You know..."

Leanna just smiled and unclipped the thick velvet rope blocking the stairwell, "Shoo! Up with you! You only get five minutes, the next tour starts in ten." I smiled my thanks to her and dragged Riley up the stairs to the lens room.

Just before I got to the top with a giggling Riley in tow, I got lost in a memory. "I had tripped on the stairs here and skinned my knee back then. I started to cry and my dad had picked me up and carried me the rest of the way. Then sat me here." I pointed at the bench by the window overlooking the Sound, with a wistful smile.

"My tears stopped immediately when I saw the majesty of Puget Sound from this vantage point, with Whidbey Island raising from the water on the horizon like a leviathan. It was then that I knew that my dad was sharing something more with me than just a tourist attraction." I confessed.

I sat down with her on the bench and I loved the childlike amazement in her eyes as she looked back to the lens then out across the waters. I let go of her hand and instead snuggled into her, my head resting in the crook of her neck, inhaling her scent. She put an arm around me and we just sat there, being with each other, watching the horizon until I heard a voice being cleared at the bottom of the stairs.

"Time's up Riley," I whispered.

She looked down and kissed my lips gently, our lip gloss sticking a bit as she pulled back. "Yup." She smiled.

We walked back down the stairs to a smiling Leanna. She hugged each of us saying, "Don't be a stranger... either of you."

I grinned. "Thank you, Lea. It meant a lot."

Riley chimed in, "Yes, thank you so much. It was great to meet you."

We wandered back to the car and hopped in. I fired a childlike smile at her. "Ok, next stop, the horizon!" This rewarded me with a grinning eye roll and a cute response, "Lead on oh cryptic one." I started up the car and drove us down the block and into the line for the Clinton/South Whidbey Island ferry.

I shot Riley a mischievous smile to which she snorted and we put on some loud music to sing along with as we waited. A girl band of course. The ferry arrived and I fished out a pass from a stack of them in my purse as we drove on, getting a snicker from my brunette beauty and a 'you know a guy' look from her. Then we drove onto the ferry's car deck and parked in our line. I reminded her to put on her jacket then we got out and I ran around to grab her hand and drag her smiling self up the stairs onto the observation deck.

As the ferry started moving away from the dock I released her hand and put my arm around her waist and leaned my head into the crook of her neck as I spoke wistfully, pointing at the island in the distance. "When my mom and dad first took me on this ferry, my mother pointed at the island and said, 'The horizon is our gift, see how the island seems to grow right out of it as we approach? That's just for us, it is greeting us, opening its arms to us, excited to show us the wonders it holds. You ready to see what it has to offer?' As a child, I remember being filled with awe, as I nodded at her. So now I gift it to you Riley."

I looked up into her twinkling eyes and she leaned down to kiss my forehead with a soft, butterfly inducing smile, saying, "You are certainly something else, Cryster. Thanks for sharing this with me. I've never thought of my destination that way whenever I took the ferries in the past. It's a new perspective. Now it feels like flying for me." I bit my lower lip and twirled my ponytail as she said that.

We hugged then I spotted something in the water shadowing beside the ferry and pointed excitedly as an Orca whale breached the water's surface.

"OMG! I love when the whales follow!" Riley chittered with a broad grin. We spent the short trip watching the whales play as we approached the island's embrace, smiling and pointing like we were little kids.

We spent the next hour driving the length of the island, talking about my childhood and the things my family did on the island.

We took in the spectacular views of Puget Sound and the Strait of Juan de Fuca. I relayed the story of the Saratoga Passage as we drove through it.

Then I was getting excited as we approached Deception Pass Park and she picked up on it and asked, "What's up Crys-munk?"

I grinned at her as I pulled into the car park before Deception Pass Bridge and replied cheerily, "This!" I hopped out of the car before she could say anything and ran around to her side and opened the door for her.

I don't think she could have got rid of her grin if she wanted to, before she could get out I murmured, "You're so beautiful," and leaned into the car to give her a passionate, but short kiss, laughing at her stunned look as I grabbed her hands and dragged her out of the car.

I was dragging her behind me as we made our way to the bridge. I stopped at the walkway onto it and released her hand. "Lunch awaits, my lady." I bowed and gestured toward the bridge. She smiled and bowed her head slightly and regally started the march across the steel trestle bride, one hundred and eighty feet above the water, me hustling to her side. She looked around as we walked. "Now I *DO* feel like I'm flying. This is spectacular, I've never thought to do this."

We held hands and just marveled at the view in a comfortable silence, just soaking everything in, just soaking each other in. As we approached the end of the quarter mile stretch to Pass Island, I spoke up, "This is where my parents told me, 'You can now tell people that you walked across the ocean from one island to another.' I was amazed and in a little bit of awe, kids see things like that with a little more wonder than adults. So now... you can say the same. Welcome to Pass Island!"

She looked at me with twinkling eyes as she spoke softly, "I feel as though I am seeing all of this through your eyes as a little girl." I smiled and grabbed her hand as we reached the small car park and dragged her off to the side, making our way into the trees past the observation point. "Where are we going?" she giggled to me.

"Here!" I said bouncing on my heels and looking into her eyes as we arrived at a checkered blanket with a picnic basket on it. I gestured grandly with my hands, "Lunch your highness!"

She chuckled, "Stealing a page from my book I see."

I grinned and started twirling my ponytail end and biting my lower lip as I replied, "I told you I got some ideas from our last date."

We had a fun time with our picnic lunch. Talking, chatting, laughing and feeding each other. We just enjoyed being close to one another. Somehow it ended with me in her arms in a steamy make out session that I didn't ever want to end. Her lips were so soft and talented, her arms so possessive. Her tongue owned mine when we deepened the kissing, I happily ceded dominance to her.

But then she broke us out of it, not making eye contact and said softly, "Maybe we better get back to the car."

What did I do wrong? I looked at my shoes and nodded. We cleaned up and made our way back to the bridge with the basket. Riley didn't say anything the whole way back to the car, and I was too scared to say the wrong thing. She looked deep in thought.

After stowing the basket in the trunk, we got into the car and I hesitated with the key in the ignition then said softly, scared to make eye contact, "Are you mad at me? Did I do something wrong?"

I chanced a glance at her as she exhaled, looking at the ceiling of the car and running her hands through her hair and saying, "No, I'm sorry. You are sharing your childhood memories with me and here I am ruining things. I'm thinking too much."

I placed my hand on her's and felt her tense for a second like she was debating on pulling it away, but then she laced our fingers.

She looked over at me and raised my chin with a finger so our eyes met. I missed those sparkling browns since the picnic. Then like a switch was flipped, her mood changed and she was smiling again. "This has to be the weirdest 'date' I have ever been on, but surprisingly one of the best."

This brought my smile back out of its temporary storage spot and back onto my face as I released her hand for a moment to start the car.

She asked, "What's next?"

"Home," I stated, taking a deep breath as I pulled out onto Highway 2 and across the bridge toward the Interstate 5 interchange. "That was what I wanted to share with you, Riley. Only Bevi knows about these trips with my parents; she was on them enough as we were growing up. But there is just something about you that makes me *WANT* to share."

She bit her lower lip then replied, "That means a great deal to me. Thanks, Cryster." Then she squeezed my hand and reached for the iPod, cuing up, to my surprise, some girl bands. Sparking off another hour and a half of improve karaoke and laughter with us on the ride back.

I pulled up to her loft at 3:00 and stopped at the curb. She leaned over and gave me quick peck on the lips. I could still feel her lips on mine as she started typing something on her phone then said, "Thanks! This was really fun and I loved the memories you shared. They made me look at things I normally take for granted in a different light."

I just gave her a tiny wave, still cooling down from her quick kiss as she got out.

She made a grand gesture hitting her phone's screen with a finger. My cell buzzed *[bored]* She was grinning at me through the windshield as I typed back *[get in]*. I heard her laugh as she hopped back in.

"What took you so long?" she giggled out to me as we made our way back to my place.

Chapter 9 – It all goes to Hell

We hit a movie rental kiosk on the way to my condo, and paid with some free rental coupons I just happened to have. This of course gaining the prerequisite smiling eye roll from Riley. Then it was off to the market for some wine. I don't think we spent more than five minutes not laughing and gossiping.

At one point I asked about Silent Bob's geeky call sign, and found out that it wasn't what I was thinking at all.

Riley had laughed and said, "Her name is Roberta Valentine but she likes to be called Bobbi. She had worked with her uncle Stuart's outdoor outfitters and mountain tours and guide shop since she was like twelve. When she grew up, her business chops were second to none right out of college and she was a whiz at investing and was already accumulating quite a tidy nest egg."

She smiled in reflection. "When Stu's business was on the brink of bankruptcy a few years back, Bobbi stepped up to fund it and lend financial and business advice. Everyone in the industry knew that she was the silent partner that saved the business, and all the regulars at the shop did too. They all started calling her Silent Bob."

Then Riley's face fell, it made me want to hug her as she

continued. "When Stuart passed away all the regulars urged her to take over the business, since she had helped resurrect it and made it better than ever. She changed the name to Silent Bob's Cascade Experience and the rest is history."

Then she tilted her head at me and smiled. "Her skills kind of compliment yours. Where you excel in networking and coordinating things to go smoothly, she is on the execution end. She can pull some rabbits out of her hat and get things set up in the mountains on next to no notice."

I grinned, "Like a picnic in the woods." She nodded with a conspiratorial look.

Then my smile faltered as I asked, playing with my ponytail nervously, "So why did you guys break up?"

She looked contemplative. "I think it came down to the fact that I was more of a hookup and have fun kind of girl, and she wanted something more substantial, a relationship. At that time I wasn't ready for that. But the past few months I've been seeing a change in myself. Like maybe I'm tired of the disposable relationships and want something more myself."

"With her?" I almost whispered hoarsely. Was I jealous?

She quickly replied, like she was worried about my response, "No. No, we had our time together. It's not like that anymore. We've moved beyond that and are great friends and help each others business out. Kind of making our own mini Cryster-network." She winked at me, proud of herself for coining a new term for my marker system. I couldn't help but laugh and smile at her child-like grin.

We made our way back to the condo and parked the car, then walked hand in hand into the lobby and up to my place. Just as I was opening the door, she leaned in playfully and pecked me on my lips and pushed her way past me. My automatic response was to curl my toes and bite my lower lip to fight the heat inside me as I watched her sway her way to the kitchen to put the wine down on the counter.

We had just got settled in on the couch under a blanket with our glasses of wine, some chips and cheese cubes, and cued up the first movie when the condo door swung open. Bevi trudged in like she was exhausted and deflated mumbling, "Work sucks! Must... shower... day's... stink... away..." stripping clothing off between words as she walked to her room, totally naked by the time she closed her door.

Riley and I shared a blush and a laugh. I shrugged, "That's Bevi for you."

Riley crinkled her nose as she laughed out, "I never really thought there were people in the world who had no modesty until I met her."

I grinned as we turned back to the movie and replied, "That's all part of her... unique... charm."

For the next half hour I spent more time snuggled up against Riley tracing little circles on the exposed skin of her abs below her shirt's hem and studying her eyes than watching the movie. She spent most of that same time rubbing the back of my other hand with her thumb and staring back into my eyes.

Then Bev's door opened and she wandered out, clean and fresh, and stood in front of us and struck a pose. Looking at Riley and grinning like an idiot. "Look Jane! Clothes!" Motioning down to the oversized t-shirt and boxer shorts she was sporting.

This got a snort from Riley. "Very good Beverly. And Cryster here didn't think you could be trained!"

We all shared a laugh and Bev laid down on the couch with her head in our laps. "Cheese me, daahlings!" She opened her mouth and Riley smiled in mirth as she dropped a cheese cube into Bev's waiting mouth.

Bev grinned and sat up then stood to head to the kitchen, calling back, "So what are we watching?" I spoke loudly over my shoulder toward the kitchen, "We have an assortment of chick flicks and action films." This got the expected reply I cringed and waited for, "Ooooo nice! Boobs and booms!" This elicited a giggle from Riley.

A moment later Bev returned with a full glass of wine and sat at the far end of the couch, giving us a little space. I smiled a thank you to her for that to which she winked back and took a huge gulp of her wine. I was about to say something when my mind went blank as Riley started cupping and gently stoking my breast over my shirt under the blanket. My hand finding its way into her pocket.

By the end of the first movie, we were starting to get into some heavier petting... with me trying hard to breath normally so Bev didn't catch on. Riley knew she was in full control and I gladly ceded it to her, she pretty much owned me on that couch.

When Bevi got up to switch the DVDs out, Riley took her hand out from under the blanket, and looked at me with an unreadable expression as thought processes finally started up again in my head. "How much longer till the first movie is done?" I whispered.

She leaned down and kissed my lips quickly with a smirk, "It's already over. Bev is cuing up the next one now."

Then as Beverly was coming back to the couch, Riley reached over to my ponytail, tilting her head at me for permission.

Bev chirped, "Sorry Jane, She's kind of 'crazy lady' about her hair. Only three people have ever seen her without her ponytail since we were like five. Her parents and I." I looked down at the floor.

Riley gently moved my gaze back to her eyes with a single guiding finger, then reached for my ponytail again. "May I?" I bit my lower lip and gave her a tiny nod, swallowing. *I don't know why I'm so scared.*

"No way." Bevi murmured, her eyes wide with surprise that I'd allow it.

Riley slid the scrunchie out of my hair and ran her fingers through my long chestnut locks and fanned my hair out across my shoulders. Her pupils dilated as her eyes darkened, she bit her lower lip then whispered in a husky voice, "Holy shit! I thought you were beautiful before... but Cryster... wow!"

I looked shyly down then started to tie my hair back up but she stopped me with a gentle hand on mine saying, "No please. Leave it down. Why do you hide it away like that?"

I glanced nervously between her and a stunned Bev as I quietly answered, "It's stupid. – When I was really young, my hair was thin and wispy and kind of stuck out everywhere, all static like. The kids in kindergarten teased me about it. Beverly had punched one of the boys in the face who had laughed at me. Then walked over and gathered my hair into a ponytail and used a little string bracelet I had made her to tie it up."

I grinned over at Bev, I had never told her this. "Then she said to me, 'There! This looks much better on my best friend!' Even back then I thought she was amazing for protecting me like a sister. If she said it looked better, well... then it must. So since then, I sorta never left the house without my ponytail... I guess it just became an obsessive habit, a safety net of sorts." I shrugged, feeling self conscious with my hair down like this.

"You never told me that was the reason, sis," Bevi said softly. I shrugged again and buried my face in Riley's neck to hide.

Riley said, "Well, I love your hair down. You should come out of hiding more often."

I looked up at her, frightened but amazed, "Really?"

She nodded down to me and kissed the top of my head and whispered, "Really."

Bev added a "Really," too.

"God, why do I feel so self conscious like this? And why does it feel like something heavy just went down? It's just hair right?" I whispered to the girls. I reached up to play with my non-existent ponytail just to drop my hand into my lap. They were both just smiling at me, so I grabbed the remote and started the movie so they'd stop looking at me. Bev helped herself to another large glass of wine.

A few minutes into the movie, Bevi was snoring on her side of the couch... I used that opportunity to turn back and start a slow make out session with Riley. *God, can this girl kiss!* We started kissing deeper and more passionately so I twisted around and straddled her and attacked her neck with my lips while my hands made their way over her shirt to gently cup and massage her breasts through it. I could feel the outline of her lacy bra with my fingertips, just fueling my fire.

Her breath hitched, and I don't think she was breathing anymore as I took control. But just like that, we were snapped back to reality by my phone ringing. Then chaos ensued. Bev sat up glancing at us, quirking an eyebrow then looking toward my phone. I jumped off of Riley, landing unceremoniously on my butt on the ground. Riley was glancing between Bevi and I with a cute blush.

Embarrassed and blushing myself, I grabbed my cell from the coffee table and stood up and answered it, walking a few paces away toward the kitchen, my back to the girls, "Hello?" I choked out. My blood ran cold, I should have checked caller ID first. I didn't want a conversation like this now. "No Earl, this isn't a good time. No... I'm busy all week. Yes. No, I don't foresee any time in the future. Ok, you too... goodbye."

I just stood there, slowing down my breathing and my heartbeat as I heard Riley ask Bev, "Who is Earl?" Beverly answered without thinking... like she always does when she is tipsy, "Oh just one of her booty calls whenever he has business in town..." her voice trailed off and I knew she was silently cussing at herself, like I was. I turned nervously as Riley stood up and started walking toward the door.

I went to intercept but she held a hand up, I saw a tears in her eyes as she spoke, not slowing down, "That's it. I can't play this damn game anymore. You made me fall in love with you to win a goddamn bet, you made me think it was real. Go back to your straight girl world, you win."

Fall in love? She loves me too? I was tearing up now, trying to grab her arm but she shrugged me away as she opened the door and walked out into the hall.

"No Riley, it isn't like that at all. Let me explain!" I pleaded as she just kept walking. "Let me drive you home and we can talk about this! You don't understand!" I yelled. She just turned down the stairs hissing, "I'll find my own way home!"

I slipped to the floor sobbing. Bevi was there holding me, "I'm so sorry, Krustallos. I didn't think before I opened my goddamn mouth!" She reached over with one hand and closed the door and just sat there stroking my hair as she rocked me while I cried.

Chapter 10 – A Month in Purgatory

For weeks I tried calling her, leaving messages, texting her. I sat outside her loft but she would ignore me. I was starting to feel like a stalker. More nights than not, I'd cry myself to sleep. Bevi would always know and would come comfort me, protect me in bed and have chocolate pudding cups ready for me in the mornings.

I was off my game. It took more effort than normal for me to arrange the parties for my clients, but I was somehow still pulling it off. Probably because I was just on autopilot, just going through the motions of a routine ingrained into me from years of practice. My mind was elsewhere, I didn't even feel satisfied negotiating trades and putting others in my debt. Her brown eyes were all I could see whenever I closed mine.

Cougar Mountain called about iFORk, but Takara refused to speak to me, instead it was some flunky who spoke with me, Hector. They would bring many of the safer animals and birds to the Urban Safari along with a ton of educational materials. At least I could still focus on iFORk, it seemed to be the only thing I still had any sort of passion for.

My heart would ache any time I saw a familiar plane with a purple wave on it flying over the city. It amazed me how I never looked to the sky much before, to notice things like that. Bev said that she had been seeing that plane for a couple years, it was like an fixture in the Seattle area. When I thought about it, though I had never paid much attention before, I'm quite sure I had seen it before, too. But now, any time I heard a small plane in the sky I'd look, just in case it was her.

I found myself going to places like Record Nirvana or to the Space Needle just to savor the memories. Is heartbreak supposed to hurt so much? My chest actually ached. This is why I never did relationships before. This can't be healthy for anyone.

There were times I felt so lonely, my first instinct was to call Riley, that realization just made it hurt that much more. So I decided to just go back to my old ways, to just call some of the guys I knew and just get a few one night stands out of my system to help me forget. But I could never get myself to pick up the phone.

It would be like betraying Riley, like cheating on her. *But we aren't together, God damn it!* I couldn't even bring myself to hit the clubs with Bevi. I would be faithful to the memory of us, no matter how brain damaged that seemed since we were never a couple. We never would be, all because I was too much of a coward to speak the truth the whole time.

I stopped taking new parties jobs for the month so I could just concentrate on the only good thing I had left in the world besides Bev, the iFORk. But it seemed the fates weren't done with their sadistic screwing with me yet.

The morning of the iFORk I got a call from Thomas Cabbot, the host of the 'Stuff of Nature' from the Earth cable channel at 9:00am. He was going to speak at the opening ceremony at 5:00pm tonight. His plane had been grounded in Missoula,Montana with some technical issue, and the only other flight that could get him here in time was booked solid.

What else could possibly go wrong in my life? The kids would be so disappointed. Thomas was a big draw for the iFORk. It was things like these famous guests that made the iFORk a memorable and special experience for these kids. I felt like crying again. My emotions are so volatile lately.

Bev came to the rescue again. "So what's the problem? Aren't you Crystal friggin' James? Wouldn't she be able to salvage this somehow? What would she do?"

I needed that slap to the face. I smirked meekly at her. "Well if Crystal were here, she'd make the best of the resources she has available to band-aide the problem."

Bevi grinned. "Well then, hop to it girl!"

I called Cougar Mountain and spoke with Hector to see if I could get one of their zookeepers to speak at the opening ceremony tonight. It would mean more exposure for them, and the kids could hear from an actual zookeeper. It wasn't Thomas Cabbot, but it was still a cool thing for the kids.

I cringed when I heard on the television that news of the guest speaker change-up had been leaked. *[[Thomas Cabbot, host of Stuff of Nature is marooned in Missoula, Montana and won't be able to attend the iFORk opening ceremony. The iFORk has always been on shaky ground, being a non profit venture. Without draws like Thomas Cabbot, the future if the iFORk festival is seems unstable. It was the brainchild of local resident Crystal James. But in a society driven by profit, it has always been a nice pie in the sky idea that looks to be proving to be just that.]]*

What the hell? They make it sound like iFORk is failing! I frigging hate the news media. They try to sensationalize everything. iFORk isn't just an idea, it is an ideal. People helping people to help others. *THAT* is what society strives for! I just shook my head at their audacity.

Bev had to talk me down from my angry internal rant. "Whoa!

Unclench those fists, Rocky! The reporters are just idiots trying to make a story out of nothing, Kru. IFORk isn't going anywhere, sis."

I flickered a smile at her. "It's scary how well we know each other sometimes, Bevi."

She snorted back, "Well, get your head in the game and lets make this the best iFORk yet!" I nodded and we walked out of the condo to get down to Lake Washington to finish setup of the party.

There were already hundreds of people with their kids lined up at the gates, we were still hours from opening. I got a little thrill seeing how excited some of the children were. It reminded me of some of the magical times I had with my parents as a kid.

The park we were holding it at was surrounded with a fake, sharp wooden post barrier that resembled the village from the King Kong movie, lending a lot of ambiance to the festival. From the inside, the view of the city was blocked off on three sides, giving it a real safari feel to it, leaving a low wall by the lake. The view was breathtaking. I was hoping that this would give that same magical feel I remember to these children.

I was happy with the assortment of animals I had sourced

from about five different locations. I almost giggled when I saw the camel. But the most impressive group of animals came from Cougar Mountain Zoo. *And there were reindeer!* I put my hand on my chest in memory of that day with Riley, feeling my heart speed up.

I went past all the vendors. The food smelled heavenly. Mrs. Z was there with her oven. There were plenty of souvenir wagons and for the people who couldn't afford much; free gifts like animal coloring books and balloons for the children. I smiled when I saw Mike setting up in a safari guide uniform. He had a bunch of stuffed animals to juggle. He sent me a small smile and wave which I returned.

After helping a few new people get sorted out and set up, Bevi and I made our way to the stage area. The gates had opened and people were filing in, gathering around the stage area. It was getting close to kick off time of the festival. I walked up to the extremely nervous looking blonde girl in the Cougar Mountain Zookeepers uniform who was reading from some index cards and offered her a smile. I checked the time on my phone as I approached her, fifteen minutes until opening ceremony.

"Hi! You must be Rebecca Vance. I'm Crystal, I'm so glad you could make it on such short notice. This is my friend, Beverly." I tilted my head and smiled, showing my genuine appreciation for her coming. She smiled nervously back and nodded at Bev. "Don't thank me until after I speak, I'm so nervous I'm going to screw this whole thing up. I hate speaking in front of people."

I looked up in thought then met her grey eyes. "I was at Cougar Mountain a while back, and all the zookeepers seemed to have fun discussing the animals with the children there. Do you do that?"

She smiled in thought. "Yes, that's one of the highlights of working at the zoo."

I nodded back at her. "Well, that's what we are all here for today, the children. Just look at it as though you are at the zoo, talking to all these wonderful kids in a big group."

She tightened her neck and shot a silly grimacing smile. "Thanks, Crystal. I'll do my best. I really think it is a great thing you are doing here."

I smiled and nodded and was about to wish her luck when I heard a commotion behind us. I turned around to find Thomas Cabbot striding up to me with a grin on his face, flanked by a bunch of iFORk people.

The huge 6'-3" brown haired man, who appeared to be chiseled in stone, stopped in front of me and offered his hand. "You must be Crystal James! I'm very pleased to meet you finally! Am I too late to speak?"

I was shaking my head in shock. "No... no, not at all. I thought you were stuck in Missoula." I glanced over at Rebecca who was breathing out a huge sigh of relief.

He smiled. "No, the pilot you sent for me got there in time."

I screwed up my face in confusion and grabbed my ponytail and started fidgeting with the end. "Pilot?"

He nodded. "Yes, she was quite lovely and professional. She really pushed that little purple plane to make it back here in time."

Now I was not only shocked but stunned... Riley did this? I felt my heart start beating again. I didn't care that she wouldn't speak to me just then, because at least I knew that in some way, she still cared a little. I tried to play it off. "I wasn't sure she'd get to you in time. It is wonderful that you did! Though I would like it if both you and Zookeeper Vance could each speak, I'd hate for her to get all prepared for naught. It would mean the world to the children."

He smiled at me then at Rebecca who was giving me a "Why would you do this to me?" look that just made me wink at her. He was charming and slightly bowed to her as he said, "I wouldn't have it any other way."

I shook his hand and Rebecca's hand again and told them, "Well you are on in five minutes. I'm going to go up front to watch. Thank you both for this." Then I strode away with Bev in tow.

Their opening presentations went amazing, Thomas was a fountain of charisma and kept the audience captivated and engaged. When Rebecca got on stage, he stood bedside her, offering moral support and urging her on with his smile. She started a little rough but as she looked around to the sea of enthralled children she loosened up and gave a brilliant speech.

If I wasn't mistaken, Thomas and Rebecca shared a certain chemistry as they left the stage together. I smiled a little at this thought. Nothing got past Bevi either. "Looks like we should avoid the backstage area doe a bit huh, Kru?" she said with an evil crooked smile on her face.

I slapped her arm with a little smile. "You are so bad, Bev!" We shared a chuckle and looked around. The place had exploded into a bustling party atmosphere. Kids were pointing at the animals, and the petting zoo areas already had huge lines by them.

"Looks like it's a hit, sis." my tall redheaded friend said with pride.

We wandered around for a couple hours, then I noticed a distinct plane with purple wingtips lazily approach and loitered over the lake for a while. I sent a thank you from my heart out toward the plane as I clasped my hands together and raised them to my lips in silent prayer. Then I texted *[thank you]* to her with a tear threatening to fall.

"Let's go home, Bev." I finally said with a slight smile. She nodded and we made our way through the crowd of one of the most successful iFORk parties yet.

Chapter 11 – Tango Alpha Three Niner

The iFORk was lauded as one of the best successes so far by the same reporters that earlier had dissed me; and it. *Fickle much, you asses?* The city okay-ed next years iFORk for October, it would be a Halloween and haunted house theme.

I moped around for the next few weeks, trying to put my life back on track, but I couldn't help feeling as though I had a gaping hole in my chest. How could one person affect another so profoundly? Especially someone that you knew for such a short period of time? This is what I've read about in all those silly stories. Love and heartbreak. Why the hell would anyone want to ever fall in love if there is even a remote chance that they could wind up feeling like me? With their heart torn out and feeling like just a half of a person.

It was an lazy Saturday around noon. I shook myself out of my funk and started working on finishing up the planning for my latest party. This upper class couple wanted a fairytale themed party for them and a 'few' friends. If you could call over a hundred movers and shakers in the Seattle metroplex a few. I knew a guy who could get a horse that looked like a unicorn with a realistic looking fake horn. That should be the last piece of the puzzle.

I pulled out my phone and dialed, "Hey, Chris, yeah it's me, Crystal. What? Don't get too excited about a clean slate, this is a small one. So you'll still owe me. Yeah, don't sound so sad, you know there's always good money in it for you. Just need Buttercup in drag in two weeks, so dust off the horn. Yeah, cool. Thanks! I'll send you the details. Have a great day!"

I slid my phone gently back into my pocket and took a breath, satisfied with my party plan. I made a couple grilled BLT sandwiches and wandered over to the couch with the food and some water bottles to sit next to Bevi to watch some mindless sitcom reruns. She always knows how to keep my mind off of serious topics.

We were laughing along with a lame show as we ate when a news bulletin cut in on the broadcast and interrupted the show. Katherine Granger, a local anchor in all her fake blonde glamor, was standing outside of a small airfield that I recognized.

[[This is Katherine Granger with XZN bringing you a special report from VanCourt Airfield in Issaquah, Washington. We've learned that about fifteen minutes ago, the air controller here at VanCourt got a distress call from a single engine plane experiencing engine trouble deep in the mountains.

The pilot announced she was going to try to get her two

passengers over the peaks to try an emergency landing on Interstate 90, but was not sure if they could get the altitude. Moments later radar and radio contact was lost, the plane is believed to have crashed in the Cascades.

The state patrol has sent out a search and rescue helicopter to look for the wreckage and has started clearing lanes of traffic on I90 near the last know location of the plane just in case.]]

My blood ran cold. Her? The pilot was a woman? And that was Riley's airfield! Bev looked at me then the television and quickly pulled me into a hug as we watched. Katherine Granger put her hand to her earpiece and turned back to the camera.

[[The tower has just confirmed they have regained communications with the plane and are patching it through on our audio.]] there was static and crackling sound then we heard an intermittent voice *[["Tower this... tango alpha three niner... to maintain altitude... cannot... interstate...]]* there was hissing and crackling for a moment and my heart felt like it was being squeezed in a vise at the sound of Riley's voice. Then the signal came in much stronger *[[Trying for the airfield, the ridge is lower there. Wish us luck.]]* Then the tower kicked in. *[[Tango alpha three niner you are cleared for approach. Godspeed and pray for an updraft!]]*

I was holding my breath and biting hard on my lip, drawing blood as the news camera swung up to the tree lined ridge above the town, zooming in, and panning from side to side along it.

Then I could make out the straining and coughing of a sputtering engine and the camera swung to the extreme northern side of the ridge where it dipped to its lowest. Just then, a familiar plane with purple wingtips shot almost straight up over the top of the ridge. The landing gear striking the treetops as it cleared in its steep climb, the plane billowing out a trail of blue smoke behind it.

The engine and the smoke stopped just as the plane hit its apogee. The plane seemed to just hang in the air for a moment. Then it pivoted silently on its wingtip before dropping soundlessly into a severe dive. A simple word [[deadstick]] crackled over the radio in her voice. I was standing now, I couldn't breath, Bev was at my back holding my shoulders as the little plane shuddered and slowly leveled out and aligned itself to the runway at a dangerously low altitude.

The tower spoke, [[Tango alpha three niner we have you on glidepath. You are coming in hot, feather out and bleed some speed.]] Riley responded, [[Roger that tower. In process.]] The plane pitched up slightly, almost into a stall, then the nose came back down just as it reached the runway. I started breathing

again as Violet touched down and Riley coasted her off the
runway into a grassy area before rolling to a stop *[[Tango alpha
three niner wheels down.]]* was her simple calm statement as the
tower kicked in *[[Welcome home tango alpha three niner.]]*

Then the camera zoomed back to Katherine. The people
standing around watching this all unfold were cheering. I was
crying as Katherine Granger stood so that you could see the plane
in the background as she spoke, *[[This is Katherine Granger live
with a XZN exclusive. We just witnessed an amazing emergency
landing of a single engine plane without power here at the
VanCourt Airfield.]].* They were replaying the clearing of the
ridge and the pullout from the dive in slow motion in a window in
the upper corner of the screen with a ticker scrolling announcing
'Exclusive Footage'.

My heart was beating fast once more as I saw the tops of the
trees being sheared off by Violet's landing gear again. I relived the
anxiety. I saw Riley helping the passengers out of the plane
behind Katherine as airfield trucks arrived at the plane. I quickly
texted to her *[im glad u r ok]* I saw her check her phone on the
TV and a moment later I got a *[thx]* from her! I put my hand to
my mouth and choked on my tears. *She responded.*

Katherine was wrapping things up, *[[XZN will keep you
updated as this story progresses. We now return you to your*

regularly scheduled programming.]] And just like nothing had happened, we were back to the canned laugh track of the sitcom. Bev turned the TV off and let me cry it out into her shoulder on the couch until I fell asleep.

I woke up on the couch under a blanket a little after five o'clock to see Bevi watching the local news. The weather was just ending and they announced an exclusive interview with local pilot 'Jane' McKay coming up after the break.

"Sorry I was such a baby, Bev. I was just so scared," I said softly, looking down sheepishly.

She turned to me with a soft smile and said gently, "Hey, there you are... Don't worry about it, Kru. I was scared for her, too. She's a hell of a pilot from what I've been hearing today. Seems she used every trick in the book to keep them aloft long enough to get to the airfield."

The commercials ended and the anchor announced the exclusive interview again as they played the footage of the emergency landing again. My heart felt like an elephant was sitting on it as I relived the terror of seeing it. Why did it effect me so much each time I saw it? I knew she was safe now.

The scene switched to a familiar hangar, where Riley was

standing by an oil stained Violet beside Katherine Granger.

[[This is Katherine Granger with XZN with an exclusive interview with Jane McKay from McKay Air Tours. The pilot that made that amazing emergency landing here at VanCourt Airfield in Issaquah Washington today. Thanks for taking the time to speak with us after such a stressful event.]] Riley just projected so much charisma as she replied, that I melted a little *[[Not a problem Katherine. I wasn't stressed at all, I knew Violet here wouldn't let me down.]]* she said with a smile as she lovingly patted her plane.

Katherine smiled and had a thoughtful look on her face as she asked, *[[Could you tell us what happened up there?]]*

Riley nodded and responded calmly, *[[I had a couple who chartered an air tour into the Cascades. We were on the return leg of the tour when it appears that I lost a seal in the engine and we started losing oil pressure. We were still about twenty minutes out and between ranges, I throttled back and started looking for a suitable landing area, but the dirt switchback roads were not wide enough and the only paved road I could find was criss-crossed with power lines.*

I radioed in my intention to get over the south range to I90 where I'd have room to land, but I was losing power slowly and wasn't sure we could clear the ridge. Our airspeed had dropped to just over sixty five knotts by then.

So instead I followed the valleys downrange, riding the thermals and catching the updrafts by the ridges to help maintain altitude and not bleed any more airspeed. This low altitude caused us to lose radio contact with the tower for a bit. We didn't have the power to maintain a proper altitude.

When I realized which valley I was following I knew there was a low ridge to the north. The only problem was that I needed more altitude so I veered to the ridges there and found an updraft and climbed as high as possible bringing us almost to a stall before diving deep into the valley to gain as much airspeed as possible.

I opened up my baby to full throttle and pulled back hard, and we shot up the ridge at treetop level. She gave me everything she had, and that extra boost was enough to slingshot us over the ridge to the airfield. But I pushed her too hard and I lost her engine.

I rode the stall around to avoid a flat spin and got us some airspeed in a dive so that we could glide to the runway. And here we are.]]

Katherine looked at her in amazement, just as Bev and I were.

[[You say that so calmly like it is an every day occurrence.]]
Riley smiled and shook her head. *[[Well it's not how I like to end my air tours. I'd like to let your viewers know that isn't included in all my tours. But really any pilot would have done the same.]]*

Katherine shook her head with a smile. *[[That's not what we've heard from the other pilots around here. By all accounts you shouldn't have made it back to the field and should be part of a mountainside somewhere. Your modesty does you credit.]]*
Riley shrugged coolly at that.

Katherine continued, *[[So what does this mean for you now?]]* Riley laughed, *[[You mean besides the FAA investigation?]]* Katherine smiled, shaking her head, *[[No I mean your company. Is your plane ok, do you have other planes?]]*

Riley faltered for the first time but regained her composure quickly. *[[No. Violet is my one and only. She might need a complete engine rebuild. This and her downtime might mean I'll have to fold the company and return to DC. The banks won't wait for payments, and without an income, my reserves won't last long.]]* My heart dropped. Return to DC? *She can't!*

This revelation hurt almost more than losing Riley. At least now I knew she was still around. I could see her flying over the city from time to time and that always gave me a tiny sliver of hope, but if she leaves now... everything is gone.

I watched as they interviewed the passengers, they remarked on how Riley was so calm throughout the entire thing, and explained everything she was doing to them as it all unfolded. Her composure and confidence kept them from panicking the entire time. *[[Through 'thermal doohickeys' and 'updraft thingamabobs' right down to the landing. Though the last ridge certainly scared the hell out of us, the trees looked so close and were going by in a blur, the plane was shaking and straining. But even through that stall she smiled and spoke to us. Let me tell you when that engine cut out I thought that was the end of us all.]]*

They affirmed that she should be lauded as a hero. Though they may not be flying again anytime in the near future. I was so proud of her, and I didn't want to lose her for good.

I looked at Beverly with a look of confidence that belied my underlying panic. "To hell if she's going back to DC. Whether she wants to be around me or not I'm not letting her company go down. You with me?"

She gave me a lopsided smile. "Where else would I be, sis?"

God I love this tall redheaded girl. We hip bumped and sat down at the kitchen counter with for a quick dinner with our iPads out to start planning Operation Violet.

Chapter 12 – Operation Violet

Working with Bevi on this project reminded me of some of the schemes we'd come up with back in our early teens. In the eighth grade, we wanted to get a local girl band who had just signed with a label to play at our homecoming dance. It was 'Leather and Heels'... yes, *THE* Leather and Heels before they became platinum selling artists. I thought fondly of the coveted autographed albums of theirs I have in my collection now.

There were a couple huge problems. One, they were a punk band and the school didn't approve of that music. Two, how the hell were we supposed to get a hold of them? We decided on a two pronged attack, first I called in a marker from the school cook, Rhonda, who's kid I tutored for free in algebra. She made up some of the favorite dishes that the Principal, Mr. Babcock and the girl's PE Instructor, Mrs. DaTary (Who, to this day, I still believe is really a man), since she was in charge of the homecoming committee.

She was to discretely mention as she delivered the food, just how popular other school's staff became with the student's when live music and more modern music was allowed at the dances. Laying the groundwork for Bevi, who was handing out Leather and Heels fliers to the student body. They were everywhere. You'd have to be blind not to see them.

We made sure to mention within earshot of the principal how cool the principal of a made up school in California was for allowing local bands to play at the dances. And how morale at those schools skyrocketed.

I pulled in half a dozen markers from students to get them to say similar things around him and Mrs. DaTary. I got one of the cute popular girls, Bethany, who owed me for finding her some imported diet snack bars to get the school bully and his buddy to fake a brawl in the halls about how lame the dances are at the school and needed to change, while the other thought that they were fine that way, then there were more kids skipping out that they could harass at the mall.

Now that the basic groundwork for the scheme was laid, we needed to find an in with Leather and Heels. Bev remembered that my dad's buddy, Clint, was a reporter with the local paper with a lot of contacts. His son, Rich, was looking for a 45 of Jenny Lynn Preston's 'Love and Blood' extended mix that I just happened to have a copy of.

I almost called everything off then and there. "No way, Bevi! Do you have any idea how rare that is and how many favors I had to call in to get my copy!? It was a limited pressing! They are selling for hundreds now on the Internet!"

She did her famous non-logic logic on me. "Krustallos, just think about it. Would you rather listen to a reproduction of a band's music or hear the real thing live? I mean one song on vinyl or a life defining night full of songs?"

Don't ask me why I thought any of that made sense, but I found myself at Clint's house knocking on the door. When he answered the door, he smiled and asked a little too enthusiastically, "Hi, Crystal! You here for Rich?" I shook my head, he looked disappointed, then I said, "No actually, I'm here to see you and see if I can't ask a favor of you."

I slowly pulled my prized single out of my backpack and handed it to him. His eyes went wide when he realized what it was. Then he smiled as he took it, "Well, don't just stand outside. Come on in. What is it that you need?"

I was able to get the contact information for Penny, the lead singer of Leather and Heels through his contacts. But I let him know that he still owed me one, that record was the crown jewel of my collection after all.

Penny was an amusing girl, I don't think I've ever heard someone use the 'F' word as a noun, verb and adverb all in one sentence before. She listened to my story and commented about how resourceful Bev and I were to get that far, but there wasn't much she could do for us. They had a publicist now that they had signed with a label. I asked to speak with him and if she could put in a good word for me. She agreed.

The next day Bev and I got a visit from the publicist guy at my house, Nick Sebastion. My dad let him in, shaking his head realizing were were up to one of our schemes. God, he looked like a tool with his boy band 80's throwback looks and his stupid floppy hair. He couldn't have been more than eighteen or nineteen himself. But he wound up being a pretty decent guy. He explained how there was no upside to them playing at a junior high homecoming.

I had anticipated this and had already pulled in a favor from my dad's boss at the teen help hotline to contact the school and get them to donate a portion of all the dance ticket sales to the charity. *All parties win! People helping people!*

I smiled. "What if I were to say that I could guarantee local coverage in the paper AND you could get more publicity by touting that the band is supporting the local teen help hotline charity? Publicity like that is like printing money."

He had laughed at that and inquired if I'd be pursuing a job in publicity after high school. He agreed to my scheme to call the school principal after he failed to convince me that they wouldn't be receptive to the kind of music that Leather and Heels play.

Bev laughed as I smirked at him and laughed out, "As long as you can get Penny to not use the 'F' word at the dance, you'd be surprised what they will agree to."

He squinted an eye at me as he dialed Mr. Babcock's home number which I had procured by pulling in a marker from the school's office secretary, who I had located some rare hybrid flower bulbs for last month.

After Mr. Babcock readily agreed to the band playing the dance and they exchanged contact information to solidify the plans later, Nick hung up. He opened his mouth to speak, but stopped, looking between the phone, Bev and I. Then he finally spoke. "That's one out of two. How are you going to guarantee the local coverage?"

Bevi grinned smugly and handed me her phone, "You're up, Kru." I wiggled my eyebrows at Nick and dialed Clint. "Hi Clint? Yeah, it's me, Crystal. Yeah, I got them. Want to clear our marker? Thought so. How would the paper like to cover the dance that Leather and Heels will be playing at the junior high for charity? Cool... no problem. I'll have their publicist get a hold of you. You too, I hope Rick enjoys the record. Bye!"

As I hung up Nick started laughing with nothing but mirth in his eyes. "How old did you girls say you were?"

Bev grinned. "Thirteen."

Nick just shook his head and checked his back pocket then his wrist. We looked at him, wondering what he was doing, he winked. "Just checking for my wallet and watch before I leave."

We were the heroes of the school at the dance, everyone but the principal and Mrs. DaTary knew what we had pulled off. And while we were backstage where Penny and her drummer Amanda were making out, we got my Indy records and their new album signed by them.

Penny got my address and promised to send me autographed copies of any future albums the band made because she loved our spunk and, "You're gonna be a heart breaker when you grow up with those fucking awesome eyes!"

I smiled at the memory, realizing that we were wheeling and dealing even back then. We didn't have to do anything as elaborate now though. It involved more of me and Beverly calling in some of my power markers and doing some networking. I don't know how many calls ended in me saying,

"No seriously... then we're even. No I'm not shitting you, you'd be free and clear." Or the more dreaded, "No really, thanks! Now I owe *YOU* one!"

- - -

As I walked around my Violet, cleaning her up and pulling pine needles from her landing gear, I shuddered at the memory of the call from my mother this morning. She was going on and on about how dangerous flying is, and this close call just proved it. I was knocked out of my thoughts when one of the other pilots yelled out from the office to me, "Hey Jane, the guard says there's a mechanic at the gate, want him to let him in?"

I looked under my plane to him and yelled back, "Yeah Rudy, I'm waiting for a few guys to come out for an estimate." I stroked Violet's side, I really hated seeing her grounded like this, she belonged in the air.

Rudy replied, "Ok, you got it, Jane!"

I grabbed a shop cloth off my rolling toolbox and wiped the oil off my hands as a huge service truck with a rear crane and flatbed pulled up. King County Aviation? *I didn't call them did I?* They are the mechanics for the elite pilots.

A solid looking man with a crew cut got out of the truck, wearing some clean, professional looking olive drab overalls with a name badge sewn on, 'Mac'. He was holding a clipboard and a large tool bag. The man looked around then smiled when he saw me. He walked over and offered his hand. "You must be Jane. I'm here to look at your plane."

Did I call them? I called so many maybe I did. I took his hand. "Hi. Yeah this is her. I lost her engine the other day."

He smiled shaking his head in appreciation. "Yeah, I saw. Damn that was some fine flying!"

I felt the heat of a blush on my cheeks. I wish people would stop saying that... it was all Violet. I diverted the conversation. "Well, I'm on a tight deadline here, I can survive a month without her. Maybe two if I stretch and eat Ramen noodles every day. So I'm looking for estimates."

He just nodded thoughtfully and headed toward my baby's engine, calling back over his shoulder, "Ok, let's take a look at her and see what we got going on here." He deftly started removing the engine fairings.

I watched for a few minutes then I left him to his diagnostics and went into the office area as Rudy was leaving. We exchanged nods then I went looking for my notes, I seriously don't remember contacting them. And speaking of, two shops have missed their appointments this morning.

I looked up the numbers so I could call them and stress the importance of this to me. I dialed the first one and they told me that they got a cancellation message for the estimate. *What the hell?* I rescheduled. Just as I was about to dial the second one Mac walked up to the office door and knocked lightly as he walked in to announce his presence. I glanced over and my heart immediately sank when I saw the sad look on his face as he slowly shook his head.

I put the phone down. "Ok, don't sugar coat it, Mac, how bad is it?"

He took a breath and tilted his head putting a hand on the back of a chair. "Yeah, looks like you blew a main seal and she's locked up tighter than a drum now. You're two choices here are going to be a complete rebuild or an full engine swap-out."

I cringed. Damn, my two worst case scenarios. I squinted an eye, still cringing like I was about to be hit. "Ok, so what's your estimate on each case?"

He looked to be in serious contemplation as he said, "A

rebuild, I estimate you are looking at five to six weeks, and right around four weeks for a swap-out. I'd have to get it shipped in from back east."

The time frame estimate was disheartening but he he didn't answer the real question. "No, I mean cost. What is it going to set me back?"

He seemed to get agitated at this, his voice raised a little, "Hey, no way. I'm not falling back into that, no cash exchanges here! I'm paying off my debt to Elliot here in exchange for that damn crazy eye girl clearing his marker to her! I'm doing this pro bono like we agreed! I need my sport plane back! So you want the rebuild or swap-out?"

What?! Debts? Markers? Crazy eye girl? What the hell has Crystal done? "Don't call her that!" I snapped, maybe a little too harshly at him. I obviously still felt protective over that amazing girl.

He held his hands up in mock defense. "Sorry, no offense intended. She's just had this marker hanging over Elliot's head for a couple years. He loves her to death, says she's a genuinely nice person, but that debt has been eating away at him. But whatever it is, it's worth him releasing my plane back to me, and I still owe him over a hundred k on it. This repair isn't worth even half of that. I just don't want him backing out of this deal."

I was stunned, just what is she doing? My heart started beating again. *God I miss her.* I just can't play her game any more. *I wish things could have been different... real.* I snapped out of it when I realized Mac was waiting on an answer from me. "Ummm... the swap out is faster. Time is my enemy here. Is that... ok?"

He exhaled a breath of relief that I didn't know he was holding, his face relaxed visibly as he smiled and shook my hand vigorously. "Thanks, Jane! I'll get right on it. I can pull the engine today and order the replacement. Should be here in like twenty to twenty-five days. You mind if I keep the old engine to rebuild and recoup some cash?"

I shook my head, still amazed at what was happening. "That's fine... and, Mac?" He looked at me indicating I should continue with a slightly raised brow. I took a breath, "Thank you. And let Elliot know that everyone is even now."

The biggest smile grew on his face as he turned around and marched back out to work on Violet. I sat down on the god-awful orange vinyl couch in the office and contemplated what had just happened. I'm still not sure.

I looked at her last text on my phone *[im glad u r ok]* and couldn't stop myself as I cried silently. All I could think about when Violet's engine was failing is that I had to get back, so I could have a chance to see Cryster again. That was my driving force.

A moment later my phone was ringing, I checked the caller ID, it was the tower. I answered it, "McKay. What? Ummm... ok. Uhhh, yeah, have them taxi to the hanger. Thanks!" Now what is going on? I walked out to the main hanger bay door and watched a Cessna 206 touch down on the tarmac and idle its way over to our hangar.

The scraggly haired young pilot cut the engine and spryly hopped down to the tarmac. He looked my way and nodded in recognition as he walked swiftly over to me with a tense look on his face.

"Jane McKay?" He asked. I nodded and accepted his handshake and his business card. He just started speaking to me like we were in the middle of a conversation, "Ok, there she is, just call when you are done with her and I'll come get her. Fuel and maintenance is on you as agreed. Let her know." Then he turned and started walking off toward the gate.

I was getting whiplash. What the heck just happened? I

looked at his card and called out to him, "Hey! Mike! What's going on here?"

He turned back and looked almost panicked. "Oh, no way! She can't back out now. She just squared things with my wife."

I shook my head. "Mike, English! I'm a little confused here."

He looked at me like I was trying to pull something over on him. "Miss James. She said her and Robin would be even if we lent you the plane while yours got repaired. Now as much as I like that girl and her crazy sister, we hate owing people. Robin jumped at this when she offered to clear the slate!"

I was stunned again, apparently that is going to be my natural state today. "You're... lending me... your plane?" He looked at me like it was a silly question then nodded and started walking toward the front gate again to where I could see a young woman waiting with a car.

He called back over his shoulder as he went, "Make sure to let Miss James know that we upheld our part of the bargain!" I nodded at his back, not that he could see it as he walked away. I didn't know what was happening just then.

What was this? Was she just trying to clear her conscience?

Was this guilt? Or did she really care about me? Was she an angel? Did she really come from the heavens like I thought? I was so full of questions. I just looked at her text on the screen again and made my way back into the office to sit and think. I could still feel her lips on mine whenever I closed my eyes.

I was bored. My first instinct was to text Cryster. It just felt natural, and I had to stop myself from doing it multiple times absentmindedly the past couple months. I almost cried after I got her 'thank you' text after I snuck off to get Thomas Cabbot to her iFORk. I had almost convinced myself that I did it for the kids and not her until I got that message, it almost broke me.

I looked at the old HotRod magazines for a second and glanced around. With Violet down, God was I bored! I caught myself almost texting her again. "Argh!" I slapped my phone down on the table and pulled a throw pillow over my face and screamed into it. It was only four days! How did she get so far under my skin in that short amount of time? Then I resigned myself to being bored and just laid back and closed my eyes for a quick nap.

I woke up on the couch a couple hours later according to the wall clock, to a soft knocking. I looked over and sat up to see Mac standing in the doorway. He softly said, "Ok I have the engine loaded up now. I'll let you know when the new one is shipped."

I smiled at him then had a thought and asked, "Think you could give me a hand for a minute, Mac?" He smiled and nodded.

I led him back out to Violet and had him help me push her to the back of the hangar and move the loaner plane in. "Thanks, Mac, you're a great guy." This made him happy as he waved and got in his truck and drove off with Violet's heart strapped down to the bed of his truck.

The next few days were insane, I was booked up for the next four weeks with all the reservations that were called in and all the damn reporters wanting an interview. I was literally swamped with calls.

When I asked how they heard of McKay Air Tours, most cryptically said "I was recommended 'by a friend'" that they always refused to name. Others said to tell Crystal that they were even now or that she owed them one. One actually gave the name of one of my longtime customers. And one said he saw my landing on TV. So doing some quick math, two out of thirty bookings didn't come from Crystal's network.

I kept arguing with myself. Either she was just messing with my mind some more, or she was really the person I fell in love with. She seemed so genuine, but she never corrected me when I reminded her it was just a game to her. I wish I had the courage to call her and just ask, point blank. But what if she told me what I am so afraid of, that she doesn't feel anything toward me. What's left of my heart would die right there. *I'm such a coward.*

When I arrived home that night, I started hunting for some food and wound up with another one of those damn granola bars. *Just how many of these things did I buy!? They are everywhere!* My internal rant was interrupted when the intercom buzzed. I walked over and hit the mic, "Yes?" A familiar male voice with a thick Italian accent came across the intercom, "Hello, Jane, may I come up?"

I blurted, "Alessandro!" as I buzzed him in.

I stood by my open loft door and watched as Alessandro bounded up the steps two at a time, then his face erupted in a broad beaming smile when he saw me and he hurried down the corridor. He took my hand in his and raised it to his lips for a quick kiss. "Jane! You look as stunning as the last time I saw you."

He's such a flatterer! I could feel a gentle blush burning as I stepped aside, letting him step into the loft. "What brings you by

Alessandro?"

I motioned toward the couch as I turned and walked toward the kitchen. "Something to drink? Wine, beer, water?"

He smiled toward me as he sat. "A beer would be great! Thank you."

I returned and sat in the chair next to the couch as I handed him one of the bottles I was carrying. I looked a question at him as I twisted the cap off of mine, "So? Spill."

I took a swig as he opened his and chuckled out, "Well I heard through the grapevine, and when I say grapevine, Miss James... Crystal can't be far behind, that you are reinvigorating your business after that spectacularly heroic landing you made last week."

I could feel the burn of a blush again at this as he took a swig of beer then continued, "I was just wanting to personally offer my services to cater any open house or gathering you may have at your Air Tour company. The murmuring in the entertainment and hospitality circles is that you are the 'in' thing right now. Especially if Miss James is willing to collapse half of her network and markers to see your endeavor succeed. Maybe we could trade out an air tour for my services?"

"What?! Half her network?" I gasped. What the hell is she doing? That could cripple her business! That marker system *IS* her currency.

He nodded somberly. "She's called in most of her high value and prized markers. Everyone is talking about it. And nobody seems to know who this girl is that she is willing to do this for. Well, almost nobody." He winked a conspiratorial wink at me as he took another tug.

"I don't understand why she is doing this. I was just a game to her." I looked down at my feet.

He actually chuckled at this. "You don't really believe that do you? This network she has formed, of people helping people, is the most important thing in the world to her. Yet she is willing to lose it for you. What does that tell you?"

I took a deep ragged breath and contemplated what he was saying to me. He finished his beer and set the bottle carefully on the coffee table then stood up with a compassionate smile. Then he quietly said, "I see you have a lot of thinking to do. I made the offer I came for so I'll be going now and leave you to your thoughts."

I stood up in a daze and followed him to the door.

He took a half step out then turned and put a hand on my cheek. "It truly was good seeing you again, Jane. Feel free to drop by the restaurant any time you like. We will always have Crystal's table for you whether Miss James is there or not."

I smiled a thank you to him and watched him wander down the hall as I closed the door... I turned and slid down to the floor with my back to it and cried.

Chapter 13 – Zookeeper Frenzy

I woke up to the condo's intercom buzzing incessantly at 6:00am. I wandered out as Bevi came out of her room mumbling, "What the hell?" She reached the door before me and she croaked out a, "Hello?" into the intercom. A familiar voice came across.

"Crystal, open the goddamn door!" Takara screeched.

Bev looked comically offended. "I'm not, Crystal, I'm insulted you think I'm that short!" I slapped her shoulder and reached across her and buzzed Tak in saying, "204" into the intercom.

I cracked the door and wandered into my room to put my hair up in a ponytail and put some real clothes on. I heard a knock and then Bev yelling, "Come on in crazy 6am intercom buzzy person, we're getting dressed!" I heard some talking back an fourth a few seconds later.

I walked out of my room and saw Bev in the kitchen getting some coffee started and I looked cautiously at Takara who was pacing frantically in the living room. This matched her voice, she sounded mad on the intercom. The moment she saw me she started walking quickly toward me almost shouting as she hissed,

"What the hell kind of game are you playing, Crystal? Why do you keep messing with Jane's head!? Is it funny for you?"

Bevi was suddenly magically between us holding her arms out wide so Tak couldn't get to me. I was tugging frantically at my ponytail. Bev had a funny... almost dreamy look on her face when she said, "Whoa! Hold on there super hot Asian chick who's name I don't know! Wanna slow down a bit and take a seat so we can all talk civilly here?"

Tak relaxed a bit looking at me then over to the couch and stalked over to sit down, almost stomping like a little girl having a tantrum. Bev bit her lower lip and smiled at her then went into the kitchen to get three cups of coffee. I wandered trepidatiously to sit timidly in the chair beside the couch, looking at my feet, they were fascinating to me for some reason right now. Bev came in behind me handing out coffee mugs, then sat down extremely close to Tak with a grin on her face. *Bevi is such a horn dog!*

I spoke softly and carefully, "Takara, this is my best friend Beverly. Bev, this is Takara, one of Riley's friends from the Cougar Mountain Zoo."

Tak looked frustrated, trying to pick a fight. She snapped, "Who's Riley?" Bev just offered, "Jane." with a crinkle nosed smile. Takara dipped her head and blushed a little as her shoulders slumped, "Oh."

Bev shot her one of her patented lopsided smiles, "Well any super hot friend of Jane's is a super hot guest here. What can we do for you, Takara? I get bored easy so lets go with the Cliffs Notes version if you don't mind."

She turned to me as she spoke with a clenched jaw, "I just want to know why you keep messing with Jane! She cried for weeks after you two apparently had some lameass bet and made her fall in love with your straight ass! Then just when she was getting her shit back together, you go and start messing with her head again. Her emotions have been all over the board the past few days, she keeps calling me in tears! Babbling something about being bored but not being able to call you."

I opened my mouth to speak but Bevi jumped in, her temper overriding her obvious attraction to Tak and her voice raised a bit. "Messing with *HER* head? Jane was the one that strung my girl along then just dumped her and refused all of her calls! I had to weather, and still am weathering Crystal's broken heart! Even though Jane *STILL* won't speak to her, Kru here is doing everything, and I mean *EVERYTHING* to make sure that Jane stays in the area. Just so Crystal can hold onto a tiny sliver of hope that Jane actually did care about her!"

I stood and put a hand gently on Bev's shoulder to stop her rant. Then I moved from the chair and sat on the coffee table facing both girls, then almost whispered, "Tak, I don't know what Riley believes, but that first night at Ballyhoo, I fell so madly and deeply in love with her that it physically hurts me not being in the same room as her. I was so afraid that I'd lose her after this stupid bet we made had run its course. And she kept bringing up to me that it wasn't real. I was a coward, too terrified to tell her the truth about my feelings and watch her walk away. Yet that's what she did anyway."

I took a ragged breath as the tears started freely falling. "I feel like I'm only half a person now without her. Like someone just tore a hole in my chest. I almost died when I saw her on TV making that landing. Then she spoke on TV of leaving to DC if her business failed! I couldn't let that happen... I need her. Even if it is just seeing Violet in the sky, I had hope. So even though she doesn't want to see me, I'll still do everything in my power to see that she is ok, and that she doesn't ever leave again."

I was openly sobbing now and felt two sets of arms engulf me into hugs. I blinked through my tears to see both Bev and Tak holding me. Tak was speaking, "Shhhh... shhh... it's going to be ok, Crystal. I didn't know. You and Jane are such idiots. We can fix this. This is the granddaddy of miscommunication here."

Bev bit her lower lip. "Hey Takara, you're kinda hot when you're calling my BFF an idiot."

Takara giggled and shyly, lowering her head as she said, "Call me Tak, Beverly."

As we all released the hug, Bevi shot back, "Bev."

We all sat on the couch with Bev between us. I tried to regain my composure as Tak spoke like she was a professor in a lecture hall, "Ok. Let's state some facts here so we can all get on the same page. One, Jane is madly in love with hot eyes over there. Two, Crystal is so in love with Jane it hurts. Three, they both thought the other didn't think what they had was real. Four, Crystal has a hot redheaded roommate. Five, Crystal is apparently as straight as a pretzel. Six, Jane's name is really Riley. That all sound about right to everyone?"

I laughed a little at this summation as Bev blushed a little. *Tak is a funny girl.* I spoke up sheepishly, "Sounds about right except for number four." I dodged the expected arm slap from Bev with a grin as I continued, "I am so gay for that flygirl goddess." Then I perked up a bit. "Lets discuss this over breakfast shall we ladies?"

They followed me into the kitchen. Tak sat on an offered

stool. Bev automatically grabbed three bowls and spoons as I walked to the refrigerator and pulled out the milk. Then Bev reached into my secret spot in the cupboard and pulled out the Fruit Loops with a cheesy grin on her face as Takara laughed at us. Bev poured the loops of awesomeness and I poured the milk. Then I put the milk away as Bevi refilled the coffee cups. Then we sat down at the same time and grabbed our spoons.

Tak grinned as she shoveled some sugary loops into her mouth, spitting out a muffled, "You guys know that was kind of freaky how in sync you just were."

I giggled and shrugged. "Comes with knowing someone since you shared diapers."

Then Bev chimed in, "So Taaak..." she said her name seductively, "...how we going to fix our girls? Inquiring minds want to know!"

I looked at them and raised my hand like I was back in school. "Ummm... why don't I just call her. Tak you can tell her it was a misunderstanding of epic proportions so she'll take the call."

She was just shaking her head. "Words, just words." Then she got distracted when she glanced at me. "You sure those aren't contacts?" Apparently she has a short attention span. She shook herself out of it and back to the problem at hand. "You need to show her, not tell her. We need something that will show her this isn't just a game or a straight girl experiment or anything."

I looked between the two girls that were apparently having eye sex with each other. I couldn't help but smile at them. Bevi never acts like this, even when she was with Lori.

Then I had an epiphany while tugging at my ponytail. "I'll lose." I stated simply. This got two sets of confused eyes to swing to me.

"Huh?" they said in unison.

I smiled like it was the obvious solution. "I'll lose." I repeated. "You two will need to get Riley to the Ballyhoo Saturday night at 8:00."

Then I started unveiling my plan. Causing shocked nods of understanding and giggles of conspiracy from the two girls that I just noticed were now holding hands. *I wonder if they even know they're doing it.* This got a smile on my lips as we laid things out. Everything would come down to timing.

It was getting time for both Bev and Tak to go to work. We said our goodbyes to Takara at the door then Bev started stripping and wandering toward her room to put her uniform on. I heard her call out, "Sooooo... Kru, what do you think of Tak? Like, ummm... you think like maybe she'd, you know. Want to go out on a date possibly?"

I laughed at her sudden shyness so decided much teasing was in order. "I don't know, she's really not my type, Bevi."

Her voice was almost shrill, "No! I mean for me you bitch!"

I laughed again. "I'm thinking it is quite possible since I was expecting you two to start going at it in the kitchen at any moment."

I heard her chuckle. "Cool. Well after we get you and your girl back together, I might just have to ask little miss Asian 'I'm So Sexy I'll Melt Your Eyes' on a date then."

I snorted and she wandered out and I already had her coffee ready for her. We hugged and she called out as she was closing the door, "Don't worry, Kru, this is going to work."

I smiled to myself and started making some calls. This wasn't complex, it was probably my simplest plan ever, but I still wanted it to go perfectly. There was no room for errors this time. I felt my stomach fluttering in hope. I wistfully touched a finger to my lips... I could still feel her kiss.

- - -

After a day of planning and daydreaming of Riley, I almost laughed when just after five the intercom buzzed and I answered it then let Takara in again. As soon as she walked in her eyes started scanning around then spoke rapid fire, "Hi, Crystal. How are you? You get everything set up? Umm... so is Bev around?"

I started laughing and smiling at her. "No, but she'll be home from work any minute, make yourself at home." Then I couldn't help myself, "You two really got it bad for each other." You could probably have seen her blush from outer space as she quickly made her way over to the couch.

I wandered to the kitchen and called out, "Coffee? Wine? Beer?" She almost immediately said, "Beer, please." I swear to God that she almost sounded like a pleased chipmunk there.

I brought out three bottles and handed her one and placed one on the coffee table as I took a seat, leaving a large gap between us on the couch. She looked at the third one in confusion and glanced at me... I tilted my head with a tiny smirk and silently held a finger up. A moment later the door opened and I twisted my finger and pointed at Bev wandering in staring to strip and wander to her room with her customary, "Work sucks! Must..."

She stopped mid sentence when she glanced over and saw Tak. "Whoa!" my blushing redheaded friend uttered then quickly grabbed her discarded shirt from the floor and ran into her room. Tak and I looked at each other and cracked up.

About thirty seconds later Bevi emerged with a grin, in a tank top and jeans as she crawled over the back of the couch and inserted herself between us. She reached over to grab her beer. "Hi, ladies," she said as Tak and I busted up laughing again. *Eeep! I think some beer shot out of my nose!*

Tak bit her lower lip and lowered her eyes shyly. "Hi, Bev." This got Bevi to bite her lower lip in return. I couldn't help but smile at how frigging cute they were together.

Bev and I shared a silent look. Food! I was thinking Indian takeout but she wanted pizza, I could see how the argument would play out to its logical conclusion. Bev smirked in triumph... I reached for the phone while Bev switched on the TV and grabbed a blanket to share with Tak. I was in the middle of ordering pizza when Tak chuckled out, "There's that freaky in sync thing again. I think I like it." We all shared a chuckle and waited for our gourmet dinner to arrive as we watched a chick flick.

After the pizza arrived and I used one of the discount coupons that Bev had scored us a couple months back, I spent much of the movie sitting back and flipping through pictures of Riley and I on my cell as I nibbled a slice. I was of course pretending not to notice all the movement below the blanket on the other end of the couch. Then it hit me. *My God!* Bevi had to have seen it when Riley and I were doing the same. I blushed in embarrassment.

I faked a yawn and said my good nights and wandered into my room, stifling a giggle toward the girls. Then I laid down on my bed, staring at the ceiling and contemplating the busy day I had planned for myself tomorrow.

For the first time in two months, I felt a ray of hope cutting through the storm cloud above me. I whispered into the air, "Good night Riley," before the first pleasant night's sleep I'd had in weeks claimed me.

- - -

Morning rolled around and my 5:00am alarm was chiming on my phone. I felt like a zombie being up this early, but I needed to be for the call back East that I had to make. I was dreading this, I don't know how I would be received.

It went surprisingly well, my heart was beating out of my chest for the duration of it. But now with an agreement to meet me tonight, I had to get ready and pack my carry on bag. I dialed my parents after my shower as I packed. After apologizing for waking them up early I explained things and they thought it was a marvelous plan. That was the last link in the puzzle.

I walked out of my room and stopped when I saw Takara standing at the counter shoveling some of my Fruit Loops into her mouth with another two bowls on the counter. She was wearing nothing but one of Bev's belly shirts and some of Bevi's little heart panties. I grinned and rolled my eyes at her. She was grinning innocently and blushing.

I turned as I heard Bev speaking from her room as she was walking out, wearing just her bra and matching panties. "Taki hon, you got breakfast ready?" She grinned sheepishly when she saw me, "Ummm... hi, Kru. Takara ummm... spent the night. It was late and umm... she had a few beers."

I laughed out loud. "Oh my God, Tak! I think you tamed her! I've never seen her at a loss for words!" I was floored when, to her credit, Tak joined in on the ribbing, "Well I am a zookeeper... I'm good with animals." I snorted as Bev blushed and lowered her head saying, "Yes ma'am." Which got us all cracking up.

"Why are you ladies up so early?" I prompted as Bevi and I went to retrieve the sugary offerings Tak had on the counter for us. It was way beyond cute when Bev gave Tak a quick peck on the lips before digging in. I voiced that with my mouth full of fruity nirvana before they could respond, "Awww... I don't know if this cereal or you guys will give me cavities first." This got some loops flung at me, but it was soooo worth the blushes.

Bev chirped, "We wanted to see you off."

I screwed up my face in confusion and played with my ponytail as I asked, "How did you know she was going to agree to it?"

Takara chimed in at this point, "Crystal, I haven't known you very long but even I have figured out it is hard to say no to you." Bev just nodded her agreement vigorously.

I looked over at Bev. "Drive me to the airport?"

She nodded and grabbed her purse off the counter and fished out her keys. "Duh. You coming, Taki hon?" She stood and started toward the door.

Takara and I were clearing our throats. Bev turned back, looking curiously at us. Tak spoke up, "Clothes, baby." *Baby?*

Bevi looked down at her almost naked form then fired a lopsided grin at us and shrugged. "Oh... that."

As my redheaded friend with no modesty got dressed, Tak borrowed some pants from me since we were about the same size, Bev's were way too long.. Then she threw on one of Bevi's shirts, she buried her nose in it and inhaled deeply and grinned at Bevi. "It smells like you, now I'm going to be thinking about you all the time." This got Bev blushing. I thought it was damn cute.

As Bev drove us to SeaTac, she asked, "So why again are you going back East? Why couldn't you just ask over the phone?" I shook my head with a small smile. "Because, like Tak said, it is only words then. Showing is better than saying." Takara was nodding with pride.

We said our goodbyes on the curb and I reminded her to pick me up tomorrow at 5:00pm so she'd have to get off of work early, then I shooed them both off to work. I turned toward the terminal and took a deep breath and straightened my back and raised my head in resolve then marched into the building and toward my gate.

Chapter 14 – Ballyhoo Confessions

I was surprised at how well the discussion went with Riley's mother back in DC. She was just as charming, witty, and easygoing, and had just as much charisma as her daughter. Riley definitely got her swirling brown eyes from her mom. For a lady in her forties she was still quite the looker. *Good genes for Riley!* I smiled to myself.

After hearing me calling her Riley she had brightened and asked if she had dropped "that dreadful Jane name" only to be disappointed when I relayed that I seemed to be the only person that got away with calling her Riley in Seattle.

She shared with me how stubborn and bullheaded her daughter could be. Though she did mention how stupid both Riley and I were for not seeing the obvious standing right in front of us. And I did feel stupid.

She thought my idea was "grand" and agreed with everything. Besides, "If my Ri-ri-girl won't come to her mom, then I'll just come to her!" I genuinely liked this lady.

She insisted I stay Thursday night in her guest room instead of a "stuffy old hotel". Then in the morning she packed her luggage for the four day excursion. One call to a taxi service later, and we were on our way to Reagan International for our flight back.

On the plane, we discussed Riley's childhood, skipping over the difficult spots. "Those are for her to share with you," she said. The conversation and chit chat flowed easily. *Must run in the family.*

She mentioned how she could understand her daughter falling for, "Such a wonderfully charming conversationalist with your mesmerizing eyes!" I was blushing at that of course.

Bev and Tak met us at the baggage claim. Well, sort of. They were making out on one of the benches there with people staring at them everywhere. We walked up to them grinning. I cleared my throat and they pulled apart quickly and stood looking sheepish.

"Ariel, I'd like for you to meet my very immodest friends, Beverly and Takara. Ladies, I'd like you to meet Riley's mother Ariel McKay."

Bev put her hand out to shake and was engulfed by one of Ariel's warm hugs, then she repeated it with Tak. Both girls were beaming as she said, "It is a pleasure to meet you girls."

I caught Bev holding back from Ariel a bit and mouthing,

"MILF" with wiggling eyebrows to Tak as we walked out to the parking structure. This got her a tandem slap on her arms by Takara and myself.

The slight smirk I saw on Ariel's lips as I caught back up to her, indicated to me that she knew what was going on behind her. I was embarrassed for Bev since she doesn't have the common sense to be embarrassed for herself. But at the same time I caught myself smiling at Ariel again. She's so bad! She really was like Riley, I thought as I shook my head.

"You're terrible you know that?" I whispered with a grin, and she actually laughed out loud and bumped my hips as the girls caught up with us.

Beverly tried to get me to drive, I snorted, "No way, Bevi, we have to split you two up on the ride back or you'd be doing it in the back seat."

Ariel got in the front passenger seat giggling, and I slid into the back seat and turned to Takara and told her, "I don't know what you did with the old Bev, but only one other time in her life has she ever been with a girl for more than a night. And that last time, I didn't approve. But with you, I definitely do. She's smiling all the time now. Thanks Tak."

Tak was blushing. We all took turns asking Ariel things about herself, Riley, and DC as we made our way back to the condo. When we arrived, my parents were already there. Lots of hugs and kisses and crying and introductions later, I couldn't believe how well they got along with Ariel. I was smiling smugly a little when Bev introduced Tak as her 'girlfriend' to my parents. My mom just gushed over them.

Takeout was delivered and after a fun night of discussing Riley and my relationship in detail, and giving the specifics of my plans, I handed the keys to condo 201 to the "adults" for them to stay there. The owner was on an extended vacation and he owed me a favor so he said I could borrow it for the weekend.

I sat in bed awake until past 2:00am, I couldn't get to sleep. Bev must have known, she always knows... she wandered in and asked, "Snuggle time?" I nodded, holding the covers open. She silently walked over and put my hair up in a ponytail instead of sliding under the sheets. I looked at her in confusion, she cleared her throat softly and Tak came shuffling in. I giggled and Bev slid in front of me with Takara in front of her.

"G'night girls." I whispered and slowly drifted off to sleep.

- - -

My eyes snapped open when the heat of the sun streaming in from the window hit my cheek. I started to sit up but Bev yanked me back down. "Not yet, sis." she said sleepily.

I laughed lightly at the familiar phrase and I kissed the top of her head, repeating "Just let me know when you are ready."

A few minutes later she turned back with a sly smile and played the replay game some more. She stretched again like a jungle cat, making a satisfied sound. "Ahhhh... thanks, Kru, I needed a Crystal recharge." Bev started to sit up. Just to be pulled back down by Tak mumbling, "Not yet baby."

This got all three of us giggling like schoolgirls as we got up. Bevi was lazily stripping and heading toward my bathroom when a smiling Asian grabbed her hand when Bev was down to just her panties and steered her back out of my room toward her own bathroom. Takara winked at me shaking her head at her girlfriend. "Don't worry, Crystal, I'll get her all trained up for you." This got a playful, "Hey!" from my best friend and a snort from me.

After showering and dressing, we picked up the three parents and headed down to The Pike for breakfast. I was making some calls as we ate to make sure that everything was ready for tonight.

On the way back, we stopped by the printers and I ran in to pick up the belly shirt I had specially printed for tonight.

Once we made it back to the condo, there was an almost tearful parting of Takara and Bevi. I had to remind Bev that Tak *HAD* to go since she was the last and most important puzzle piece. Without her convincing Riley to go clubbing tonight, this was all for nothing. This got me a, "Pudding?" I nodded my ok and crossed my arms like a scornful mother as she bounded off like a kid to the fridge to get her pudding cup, much to the amusement of the 'adults'.

After a fun time talking and laughing for hours, then making lunch for everyone, I left them all in Bev's capable hands so I could be alone in my room for the rest of the day to freak out. I was so scared. *I hope to God this works!* I dozed off with dreams of Riley on my mind.

At 6:00, my bed moved as someone sat on it, I didn't even open my eyes, I knew who it was. "Krustallos, time to start getting ready."

I whispered back, "I'm scared, Bev." She just stroked my hair, and pulled my ponytail out.

She responded softly, "I know, but we *KNOW* that she loves you too, sis. Everything is going to be great. You'll see."

I let her drag me up to my feet and she pushed me into the bathroom and shut the door. I heard her call out, "I'll take care of the old'uns, we'll see you there, Crystal."

I smiled, she usually reserved my real name for either serious topics like this or her humorous remarks. "Thanks, Beverly. Love you." I caught the, "You better!" as I heard my bedroom door shut.

I took a long shower, trying to relax myself for tonight. I let the water stream across me, washing the tension tension from me. Letting the fear drain away. I finally took a deep breath and turned the water off and stepped out, steeling myself with resolve as I dried off.

I wiped the steam from the mirror and took a good look at myself as I used the blow dryer on my hair. I put on my lacy white bra and matching panties then slid into my best, tightest, white low cut capri jeans. White ankle socks and my pink converse.

Then I pulled on the pink belly shirt I had picked up today, topping it with a white blouse with just the middle button done and tying the shirttails in front to both hold it closed and to show off my tone belly. I checked the mirror, then rolled up the sleeves.

Satisfied with what I saw, I then did something I virtually have never done in my life. I pulled out my dusty old curling iron and plugged it in. I spent the next twenty minutes putting my long chestnut tresses into loose ringlets. Then I gathered it all up into a sloppy ponytail and fastened it with a simple barrette. Pulling a couple locks free to drape down my face.

I moved on to my makeup. I went with heavy eyeliner and mascara with a smoky eye shadow, heavier than I normally do. Then finished off with a satin pink lipstick covered with a clear gloss, giving a creamy depth to my lips.

I checked the time. 7:00... then I spoke to myself in the mirror, "Ok, Crystal. No time to panic, this is it. Let's go!" I nodded and grabbed my purse and walked out of my room and toward the door. I covered my mouth and let out a little laugh at the note taped to the door in Bevi's loopy handwriting, "You got this, Kru! Don't choke! Luv U, Bev."

The drive into Seattle to the Ballyhoo Club felt oddly like a death march. This could go one of two ways, and boy did I pray it was the favorable one. I cruised the lot a few times until a convertible pulled out of a space and I darted in before any of the others circling could nab it. *One point for me! Is this a good omen?*

I walked past the line stretching down the block and up to Minnie and touched her shoulder. She turned and shot me a genuine smile, "Crystal! It's been months again! I was confused when Beverly went in before you with a group in tow."

I grinned at her. "Yeah, I'm just running a little late."

She smiled and offered her standard teasing, "Still straight?"

I wanted to start giggling when she almost fell off her stool when I replied, "No. Not so much." I had to steady her.

She looked at me with a huge grin on her face. "About damn time! So who's the lucky girl?"

I blushed and looked down shyly. "Well me... if Jane will have me." The name Jane just sounded odd coming off my lips any time I said it. But that's who everyone knows Riley as here.

"She'd be crazy not to, Crystal. Now get in there and find your girl." She motioned with her head to the club with a big grin.

I leaned down and kissed her on the cheek. "Thanks, Min."

She beamed at me as I timidly entered Ballyhoo alone for the first time. Girls in line were booing me for getting in before them until Minnie snapped her steely gaze at them. I suppressed a giggle.

I caught myself marching to the bar, it was ingrained into me after so many times being here with Bev. I smiled to myself and continued to it, knowing there was a good reason to this time. As I slid up to the bar, Maggie saw me and came running over, squealing with excitement, "Oh my God! Crystal! This is so exciting! Everything is all set up for 8:00pm. Just twenty more minutes!"

She stopped to look into my panicked eyes. "Aren't you excited?"

I shook my head. "No. Terrified. What if she doesn't want me, Mags?"

She just rolled her eyes and smiled as she responded while she poured me a shot and slid it over, "She'd be crazy not to, Crystal. Here, liquid courage." I slammed the shot back and put the glass down and she took my hand.

"It's all going to work out fine, I can feel it. Oh hey, here comes Bev with those old folks she's been towing around. Good luck, I'll have the mic ready for you at 8:00" She tilted her head toward her approach.

I gave her hand a squeeze and released it with a smile. "Thanks, Mags. You're a good friend." She winked and went back to her other patrons.

The band was kicking a fun cover as Bevi dove into a hug when they reached me. "Kru! You didn't chicken out!" I laughed ay her teasing.

My dad, to his credit, didn't seem to look uncomfortable or out of place at all as he flagged Maggie down. "Three long-necks please, young lady." Maggie came over and grinned at him and served them up. Dad handed one to Ariel and mom.

My mom was blushing at the attention she was getting, there seemed to be lots of cougar hunters around. Ariel seemed to really be soaking up the attention, she laughed and yelled to me over the music, "Maybe Ri-ri-girl has the right idea here." Then shot me a toothy grin before turning her attention to a twenty something girl and biting her lower lip like I've seen Riley do and wandering off to the dance floor with her. I laughed out loud.

Bev looked at me. "Time for one dance before showtime,

Kru! Let's hit it!" She grabbed my hand and dragged me out to the middle of the crush and we lit it up. Hands above our heads, swaying and bobbing. She knew this would loosen me up. *I love my best friend!* I laughed and pointed when I saw my parent's dancing on the edge of the dance floor.

My eyes were scanning everywhere for Riley or Takara, I couldn't find them anywhere in this capacity crowd. I yelled to Bevi, "Have you heard from Tak?"

She shook her head sadly. "Nothing in the past hour. She said it was a hard sell to get her out partying. I haven't heard from her since." I started to feel the anxiety building again.

The song ended and the lead singer caught my eye and nodded as a slow song started up. We left the dance floor and made our way to the bar. The parents were already there. I checked my phone, 7:58... just two minutes. Where is she? I kept scanning the crowd for those familiar eyes, my panic was rising.

I motioned to Maggie and she fished out the wireless mic and slid it over. Bev yelled to me, "I don't see them! You still going through with this?"

I smirked at her. "Have I ever done anything half way? I finish what I start, Bevi!" She gave me a sad smile, knowing I was right.

I jumped up onto the bar and the band stopped playing instantly pointing at the bar.

"How's everyone doing tonight?" I yelled into the mic. It was like an ocean wave as I watched everyone's heads swing back to the bar, they cheered in response, not knowing what was going on.

"Many of you know me, I'm Crystal James. My friend Beverly and I are pretty much fixtures around here." There was more cheering. I continued, "Most of you know two things about me... and no, I don't mean my eyes!" This got a laugh from the crowd. I elaborated, "One is that I value my network of markers above all else! And the second is that I'm about as straight as they come!" This got mumblings of agreement.

"I want to share a little story with you before we talk about those two things! A lot of you know Riley, well you all know her as Jane." This prompted more cheers. "Well the last time I was here over two months ago, she tried to pick me up." There was some chuckling. "I quickly explained I was straight and was just here to be Bev's wingman." I saw a lot of nods, most people knew this about me.

"Well Riley happened to imply that means I'd be a bad date anyway then." There were some chuckles. "So we made a bet! We'd each get a chance to date the other. And whoever organized the best date won, and the loser had to get up here on the bar and admit that the other made them their bitch!" This got some deafening cheers.

I waited for the cheers to die down a bit. "Well, we danced the night away after that. And you know, a funny thing happened then. I had more fun that night than just about any other night in my life. I was starting to doubt the theory that I was straight, and she laid a kiss on me that still has me weak in the knees today! If I were to base it off of that night I would have already lost the bet." More whistling, clapping and cheering erupted.

I smiled. "Well let me tell you that first date, I couldn't keep my eyes off her. At that point I couldn't have cared less about the damn bet. I had already fallen head over heel in love with that woman! It was like a fairytale. We shared some kisses that melted my soul." The crowd was going wild at this. "But then she reminded me it was just a game." This elicited a shared "Awwwww."

I took a breath. "If only I had not been such a coward. I would have told her right there how I felt. But I was terrified she didn't feel the same. We shared almost every minute of free time we had between dates together after that. I felt a relationship growing like none I'd ever experienced. Yet time after time she brought up the bet. Time after time I was a coward."

"She took me on her date and shared part of her world with me. I fell deeper in love, and my heart swelled for her. Her date blew mine away. But I was afraid she'd move on after our stupid dumbass bet was over! So I said there was no winner yet, just so I could spend more time with this fascinating woman." I was scanning the crowd, I still couldn't see her, I glanced down and saw thew supportive looks from Bev and the old'uns.

"I shared my life with her. I didn't care who 'won', I just wanted her to know... me... then maybe she wouldn't leave." I saw more than one tear stained face in the crowd as I tried to keep my voice from wavering .

"In all my fear, I didn't once have the courage to tell her until it was too late. She had left my life, accusing me of making her fall in love with her just to win an asinine game... that's the last I saw of her two months ago." My voice hitched and tears were threatening. There were sympathetic mumbles from the crowd.

"Well, if you know me you know I always finish what I started. Well, about that straight thing? I'm as gay as any lesbian can get for that Riley McKay! I'm so totally, one hundred percent, head over heels in love with that magnificent woman!" The cheers finally returned with a vengeance.

I was so nervous and filled with anxiety. I was tugging at my ponytail with a vengeance. "And I brought my parents here from San Jose, and her lovely mother from DC, to profess that in front of them!" The ladies were going wild.

"Now these are just words. I believe in deeds over words, so that second thing you all know about me... my network of markers..." I held up my cell phone and my blood went cold as I hit send on my email, "I just sent a mass email to everyone that owes me, canceling all markers!" There was a collective gasp from the people who knew me.

"This is to show that there is nothing... NOTHING that I love more than Riley. Now I'm just an ordinary girl, offering only herself to the woman she loves." I was crying openly now.

"I hide in my safety net all the time, this ponytail that you never see down, my own little psychosis. But I want to bare myself to the world for her, I pulled the barrette off and let my hair fall around my shoulders." I was sobbing now.

I untied my blouse and tore it off, displaying the pink shirt that read "Riley's Bitch" and I choked out with a smile, scanning the crowd in vane... she didn't even come. "I lost. I lost the moment she said hi. Riley McKay, the love of my life, made me her bitch!"

Everyone was going crazy as I jumped down sobbing. Ariel and Bevi were hugging me as the music started back up. I just set the mic on the bar and Maggie slid me shot with a sad look on her face and sympathy in here eyes.

I tossed it back and slammed the empty shot glass on the bar just as my cellphone buzzed. I looked down at it and stopped breathing at what I saw. Blazing away on the screen was a text message from the girl I loved *[bored]*. I sobbed again and hesitated, not knowing what to do... I swallowed my heart that had somehow made its way up into my throat and slowly typed out *[call me]*. A moment later I got another message *[turn around]*.

I steeled myself and turned around... and standing no more than three feet away was the object of my desire, of my obsession. Riley, who appeared to be sobbing as much as I was, standing next to a grinning Takara.

I put my hand over my mouth and let the tears continue to fall as I reached out to her and she ran the few steps into my arms and we sobbed into each others shoulders then pulled back and kissed with a passion that I have never felt in my life. We broke the kiss and I stuttered out, "Hey girl. Why you so bored?" There was cheering all around us and another passionate kiss from her.

I broke our kiss, gasping for air and held her at arms length. "I really love you, Riley! Please know that!"

She was nodding and crying still. "I know, Cryster. I was so stupid. I'm so in love with you, too!" I was shaking my head and crushed our lips together in desperation.

When we broke our kiss again, she released me and turned to hug her mother then grabbed my hand possessively and laced our fingers together like they should always be and said, "Mom... this is the woman I love, Crystal Melody James." Ariel just grinned at her and nodded then pulled us into a warm group hug.

I followed suit with the introductions, "Mom, dad... this is the only true love of my life, Riley Winfred McKay." We got more hugs. I glanced over and laughed through my tears and pointed at Bevi and Takara making out like their lives depended on it. Riley's eyes went wide for a second before she laughed, too.

She suddenly gave me a sad look. "You destroyed your network for me..."

I smiled, shaking my head. "But I have you, don't I?" She smiled and nodded vigorously. I smiled back. "Then I got the better end of that deal." This got me a knee buckling kiss that left me warm and tingly in all the right places.

She got a sly grin on her face and whispered in my ear, her hot breath causing goosebumps to run straight down my neck. "My place?"

I was feeling light headed now. My goddess wanted me. It was my turn to nod vigorously. And we slipped out of the club... abandoning our friends and family and not feeling any guilt over it, our lust overriding all else.

That had to have been the longest ten minutes of my life, getting from Ballyhoo to Riley's loft. Our hands always connected as she drove. We may have run a few red lights, I'm not sure... all I could see was her dazzling eyes and those lips that made me growl in hunger. My arousal was almost unbearable! *I've never felt like this in my entire life!*

We may have already been shedding clothing as we entered the door to her loft. As soon as it closed I grabbed her and slammed her up against it and attacked her delicious lips and neck. Nipping, sucking and kissing every available inch of exposed flesh. Reveling in her scent and the taste of her flawless skin.

She gasped out in arousal, "Oh thank God! I was worried you'd wind up being a pillow princess." I laughed as I tore her shirt off, literally, right down the center and started kissing and nipping my way down the luscious valley, while my hands worked on her bra clasp.

My voice sounded husky and filled with lust as I rasped out, "You're going to swear that's what you are by the time I get my fill!" Her shocked face gave way to a haze of pleasure as I claimed what I've wanted for so long.

Chapter 15 – Life as We Know It

I have never woken up so, invigorated, so... alive, in my life. I looked at the most beautiful person I had ever seen, lying naked with me, our arms and legs intertwined there on the throw rug at the base of her bed.

I stifled a giggle, well... we almost made it to the bed in our four hour marathon lovemaking session. I was delightfully sore in all the right places. Never in my wildest dreams could I have imagined the things we did with each other last night. It was a combination of something animalistic and something too beautiful for words.

I still can't believe this is real. She really loves me... we're together! I gently stroked her hair as I lazily drew featherlight tiny circles on her stomach with my fingertips. Her eyes fluttered open and she smiled softly. "What a wonderful way to wake up."

Then she looked into my face and locked eyes with me, I was getting lost in her swirling brows as she whispered in wonder, "It was real. You really are here... I love you so much, Cryster..."

I gave her a gentle kiss on the lips and laced our fingers, "I love you too, Riley."

Then I giggled. "We really should probably get to my place. I'm sure our folks are wondering where we disappeared to."

She snorted. "Or probably not." Then we both cracked up and helped each other to our feet.

She leaned in and whispered, "You sure you were a lesbian virgin before last night? The things you did to me... nobody else comes close." I blushed at this and nodded.

She led me into the bathroom and we showered... oh God what a shower... this woman is insatiable! Then we dressed for the day between touches. I put on one of her shirts. I could smell her scent on them, it was doing naughty things to me. Now I know what Tak was saying as I purred, "Mmmmm... it smells like you, now I'll be thinking about you all day!"

I shot a quick text to Bev *[on way home. 'rents mad?]* I got a quick response *[^>o<^]*. I shot back *[wtf?]* To which she replied *[scrunchie nosed wiggling eyebrows... duh kru]* I laughed. Then she sent *[dunno, they no surface frm 201 yet]*

We hopped into Riley's car and she cued up some girl bands for me and we sang the whole way home at the top of our lungs. Bobbing and swaying to the music. Our hands always connected, with my thumb gently stroking the back of her hand.

It took over five minutes to walk up the stairs of the condo as we stopped every other step to remind our lips why they were meant for each other. Riley's tongue was taking my speech last night to heart as it made mine its bitch.

As we hit the hall of the second floor I swear that I saw the girl that Ariel was dancing with last night get on the elevator with a very satisfied look on her face. Riley and I shared an "OMG" look as we made our way to the door of the condo.

I opened the door and we walked into cheers from our friends and family. Our parents, with Bevi and Tak, were all congratulating us for "Not being stubborn dumb asses." anymore. It wound up being a nice pleasant day, catching up with the folks and just soaking up "family". I didn't speak much, just about every time I did, Riley would find a discrete way to touch me and I'd clam up. *Damn, she already knows how to control me... swoon!* It was her new game.

My parents flew out that night. They caught a cab from the condo, giving all of us girls hugs and kisses goodbye. Ariel would be flying home in the morning. She did something over at the intercom, then came over and said her goodnights early and retired to 201. Was that the girl from last night again, hanging around at the end of the hall?

Bev and Tak snuck off to 'their' room and I laced my fingers with Riley and brought her slowly to my room. No words were spoken, we just got in bed and cuddled, staring into each others eyes until we fell asleep. That was a whole new layer of intimacy for me. It felt... just... right.

Morning brought the present of staring into Riley's eyes again. It felt like this was how every morning is supposed to be. I whispered, "I want to wake up to your eyes every day."

She crinkled her nose. "That's exactly how I feel." We laced our fingers and just sat there for a minute before we knew the day would have to begin.

On cue the door swung open and a super-sleepy looking redhead shuffled in and fell face down on top of us in the bed. Moments later, a super-sleepy looking Asian girl came shuffling in and fell face down on top of us too. She mumbled into the bedspread, "Mornin' girls." We all cracked up laughing then savored the last minute of silence.

The soft knock on the condo door signaled the start of the day and our return to our life as we know it. We all stood and stretched, Tak and Bev wandered out to let Mrs. McKay in while we made our way to the shower.

As we stood, letting the water flow across our bodies, reinvigorating us... I tilted my head at Riley. "You really are beautiful, you know that?" She blushed, even with the hot water flowing.

After getting dressed we entered the world to bring Ariel to the airport so she could return to her normality after the chaos of this weekend. Tearful hugs and kisses were exchanged at the terminal with a promise to visit soon.

The next few weeks were pretty rough for my professional life. Without my network, I had to start from scratch. Slowly building my web again. It took a lot more effort to plan the parties. *Is it really this hard for other people? Yuck!* But they still turned out to be 'Crystal James quality.'

I had moved into Riley's loft, leaving the condo to Bev and Takara who had moved in with my green eyed BFF. Bevi reminded me that my room was always there.

Riley was quite inventive, I think she showed me more ways to make love than has been documented in all the books on the subject. Our passion never seemed to ebb, it just seemed to continue to build. The day that Violet's new engine was installed and she was cleared to fly. Riley was in the air with her the whole day then I was walking funny for a week... with a smile.

That brings us to now. On a lazy Saturday around noon, we were sitting on the couch eating some grilled ham and pepper jack sandwiches (I had found and destroyed the seemingly endless supply of tasteless granola bars stashed all around the loft), the intercom buzzed.

I wandered over and hit the mic, "Yes?" A thick Italian accented voice responded, "Miss James!" I quickly buzzed him up without a word and opened the door a crack then made my way to the kitchen to grab a bottle of beer and snuggled back in with Riley on the couch.

A few seconds later there was a light knock, Riley looked back with a grin, "Come in, Alessandro." He joined us in the living room and sat in the chair and grinned at the beer sitting on the side table there. He twisted the lid off and took a swig.

"I'm so glad you two wound up together. You make such a beautiful couple," he gushed.

I tilted my head and smiled at him. "What brings you by our humble abode, Alessandro?"

He grinned. "Well since you two are in the neighborhood I've been wondering why you haven't dropped by. Your table is always open Miss James... I mean Crystal."

I quirked an eyebrow. "All markers were cleared, Alessandro."

He waved me off. "Who cares about that silly marker business. You two are my friends, that's why you always have a table with us. A lot of others feel the same as I do. That's why I'm here today, to invite you for dinner at the restaurant tonight."

I opened my mouth to politely turn him down, I didn't like owing anyone, but Riley beat me to it. "We'd be delighted to, Alessandro. Thank you for such a gracious offer." Then she eyeballed me, I read an entire conversation full of arguments, points and counterpoints in her eyes with the only logical outcome... I lose. "Yes, we'd be happy to have dinner there tonight." I said with a smile.

I gave her my admonishment with my eyes complete with a promise of retribution, which her eyes laughed off. Damn it... I'd only ever been able to read and be read with a look with Bev, but Riley takes it to a whole new level!

Alessandro stood and grabbed each of our hands and kissed them and called over his shoulder as he showed himself out,

"Good! I'll see you lovely ladies at 7:00." We chimed out a goodbye as he left.

I swung my eyes back at Riley and opened my mouth to speak, but she beat me to it. "No. You lost remember? You'd think the sting of defeat from just a minute ago would be fresh in your memory." I seriously giggled at her affirming all of my previous thoughts.

Then I shook my head. "I love you."

She blushed and crinkled her nose at me and we enjoyed the rest of the afternoon, chatting and laughing and getting to know more about each other again. Girl bands being played on the phonograph.

We were putting on our evening wear when a thought popped into my head. As I was zipping up her dress and kissing the back of her neck I whispered, "I want to share your world... I want to learn to fly." Her smile couldn't have been any bigger as she turned to kiss me. "Ok."

We walked hand in hand, toward King Street and Alessandro's as Riley got a silly look on her face and started humming Eternal Flame. My laugh died down quickly as I joined in. We were belting it out by the time we reached the doors to the building.

Gaining us some odd looks by people passing by.

"God, you're so much fun!" my brown eyed beauty exclaimed as we got in the elevator. "Only with you my love... only with you," I whispered. And I was lost again in her eyes.

I was barely aware of the elevator opening or Alessandro greeting us and leading us to my table. I only snapped out of it when the food came.

"You're so easy," she giggled at me.

I rolled my eyes. "As before... only with you." This got the desired blush from her. *Ha! Take th... whoa, what a smile! I lose.*

She snickered in victory as we ate. As usual, the food was over the moon good. Alessandro can cook! And I told him so when he returned to the table to ask about dessert. "This was some of your finest, Alessandro!" Riley nodded vigorously in agreement. " I don't have any room left for dessert. You Riley?" She shook her head, holding her stomach contently.

He smiled at us. "Well then, here." He handed me a gilded envelope. I raised an eyebrow and Riley and I looked between him and the envelope in curiosity as I opened it.

Inside was a single slip of paper with two eyes on it, one blue, one green. Printed on the face of it was "Crystal Currency" then "One Marker" with Alessandro's signature on it.

I looked at him and he smiled, tilting my head in inquiry. He smiled back and said, "You have been a driving force in this city for years Miss James. Your network of people helping people, all using your marker system has been beneficial for everyone involved. We all know how much it meant to you. Not just for yourself, but for all the others you brought together to make such a tight knit community based on helping each other out. Nobody ever got a raw deal from a trade. And you gave it away for the noblest of purposes."

He smiled over to Riley. "For love." He turned back to me with a smile. "We all know you used your system like currency so nobody ever had to put out cash or strain their finances. Almost everyone you ever dealt with, sees you not as a business acquaintance, but as a friend." I was misting up a bit and brought a hand to my eyes to prevent it.

He continued, "So I reject your voiding of my marker." He motioned with his head behind him. "And so do they."

I looked and all of the restaurant patrons had stood and were lining up to the table. I looked around and realized, I knew every single one of them!

Mike walked up and gave me a Crystal Currency marker with his signature and smiled and walked off, then it was Mrs. Z, Elliot, the Carmichael twins, Sam, Lucinda... the list went on. I was openly crying now, by the time it was over I was holding almost a hundred markers. Riley was hugging me as I cried.

Then Alessandro handed me another stack. "The people who couldn't make it tonight. In all, one hundred sixty eight markers."

My God, that was over 90% of my old network! Then I stood shakily and threw my arms around him whispering, "Thank you." And the restaurant erupted in cheers.

Riley and I spent the next hour wandering around from table to table, thanking everyone and chatting about how they have been doing. This ranked near the top of my list of the most amazing nights of my life, just below all the nights I've spent with my brunette goddess.

The smile on my face was there our whole walk home with a stack of markers in hand. Everything really is going to be ok... isn't it?

Epilouge

I was leaning against my Violet in my dress on the ranger's airstrip just past the north range as I looked at the four other planes scattered about the clearing with the pilots lounging around while their passengers were at the ceremony by the lake. I checked the time on my cell, fifteen minutes before we had to be there, where the hell was my wife?

Just as I finished that thought a distinctive Cessna 205 with red wingtips and leading edges, and its signature wavy red swoop on the fuselage came rocketing over the ridge. Cryster's voice crackled over Violet's radio *[Whiskey bravo five niner on approach.]* I watched in wonder as she executed a swooping dive, her wingtip perpendicular to the valley floor. *God, I love this woman, she's a natural in the air.*

I've always been amazed to watch her fly after her first solo on our honeymoon two years ago. It's almost impossible to get her out of the air now. But why would you want her out of it, what she can do up there is as beautiful as she is when I'm lost in her wonderfully hypnotic dual color eyes.

Our private channel crackled to life as Crystal broke her Scarlet into an arcing, banking swoop toward the field. *[Hey baby, I have you and Violet in my sights. Be down in a minute.*

This is just so awesome up here!] I laughed and grabbed the headset I had hanging outside Violet's door, "You better get your sweet ass down here. It starts in like ten minutes!"

I could imagine the smirk on her face when she replied, *[Oh so you want me down there huh?]* Scarlet broke into a steep, graceful dive and she buzzed the airstrip just a couple feet above the ground, then shot almost straight up in a twisting arc. *How can Crystal get her to do that?*

She rode her into a stall and went into flat spin for a couple seconds as she gathered airspeed and then gracefully coaxed her into a swooping recovery back on the glideplane and circled around smoothly to land on the dirt runway.

Damn that was some nice flying, is it wrong that that made me so hot I want to take her right here in the field? She taxied Scarlet over to park next to Violet and I as the other pilots applauded her while she cut the engine. I bit my lower lip as I watched her take off her headset and update her log on her iPad quickly.

She hopped out of the cockpit in her gorgeous dress and struck a pose for me then swooped into my arms with that childlike smile I can't get enough of. She whispered into my ear, her hot breath doing unimaginable things to me down below,

"Whiskey bravo five niner, wheels down." Now I felt like I was flying again.

My lips automatically found hers, my favorite sensation is when our lips slide together and our lip gloss sticks. We broke the kiss gasping to another set of applauds from the other pilots. I grinned at them then grabbed Cryster's hand. "Come on, Mrs. McKay, we're going to be late."

She giggled at me as we ran along the path through the trees. "On your six, Mrs. McKay!"

We broke into the clearing. Tak and Beverly looked stunning in their gowns as they stood by the minister, waving their hands to us indicating to hurry.

If they weren't so perfect for each other, the way Bev towered over Takara would be kind of funny, especially since everyone knows Tak wears the pants in their relationship.

We laughed and ran past all of our friends seated on the white chairs around the beautiful arbor that Silent Bob had somehow got here. Crystal stood next to Beverly and I stood next to Tak and gave her a nose scrunching smile.

Beverly spoke up, "Ok, preacher dude, *NOW* we're ready. Hit it." All the guests laughed. Typical Bev. She was rewarded with a nose crinkle from Takara. *Doesn't she know that only encourages her?*

It was a beautiful ceremony. I'd be lying if I said I didn't get a little misty as they said their I dos... remembering Cryster and mine. She was so cute biting her lower lip and spinning that damn seductive ponytail that she only wears to drive me crazy with desire now. She stuttered out the words, it was so adorable! But her vows brought me to tears. It is phenomenal how one person can so completely effect another with only their words.

Bev and Tak's reception was particularly fun. Mostly because I always enjoy watching how in sync Bev and Crystal are with their interactions.

Friendship like that is a rare thing. I can actually see the silent communication between the two as they plan things out seamlessly. It is so similar to how Cryster and I do it. Them tag teaming Tak with the teasing is the only time Bev can get a victory over her girl.

After the reception, we watched as the newlyweds, who couldn't seem to keep their lips or hands off of one another and all the guests were flown out on the other planes. Cryster and I had been heating up all afternoon. *God she's sexy... and those eyes!*

She kissed me so passionately I think I'll be tingling for a month then she broke it and darted to Scarlet, almost skipping. I wobbled my way to Violet still in a happy daze. She shouted over to me, giggling, "I'm calling in my marker! Fly with me!"

I grinned at her enthusiasm and called back, "Any time my love! Any time!"

Once again, I felt as though she was gifting me the horizon.

Other Books in the Music of the Soul universe...

(All books are standalone and can be read in any order)

Music of the Soul

A Deafening Whisper

Dating Game

Karaoke Queen

CPSIA information can be obtained at www.ICGtesting.com
Printed in the USA
LVOW05s1923310314

379676LV00018B/931/P